spot the
difference

JUNO
DAWSON

HOT
KEY
BOOKS

First published in Great Britain in 2016 by
HOT KEY BOOKS
80–81 Wimpole St, London W1G 9RE
www.hotkeybooks.com

A CIP catalogue record for this book is available from the British Library.

ISBN: 978-1-4714-0567-9
also available as an ebook

This book is typeset in 10.5 Berling LT Std using Atomik ePublisher

Printed and bound by Clays Ltd, St Ives Plc

Hot Key Books is an imprint of Bonnier Publishing Fiction,
a Bonnier Publishing company
www.bonnierpublishingfiction.co.uk
www.bonnierpublishing.co.uk

ALSO BY JUNO DAWSON
(Writing as James Dawson)

All of the Above
Under My Skin
Say Her Name
Cruel Summer
Hollow Pike

Mind Your Head
This Book is Gay
Being a Boy

To Samantha – you look so fine.

x

Chapter One

I hate them but they are all I think about.

The A-List.

I observe them covertly from the table next to theirs in the canteen, peeking out through my greasy hair curtains. They always look like they're having so much fun. Even in this grey canteen, a personal ray of sunshine seems to follow them around. What perfect white teeth they have. They're laughing – in a riotous, attention-seeking way – at something Rufus is saying.

Rufus, the funny one. A class clown, sure, but handsome in his own quirky way. He's dating Lucy, the delightful one, and she's sitting on his knee picking at his fries. With her white-blonde hair and big blue eyes, she's Disney's Aryan princess. I don't know why she puts up with Rufus. People – in fact everyone she comes into contact with – love Lucy and have done since we were all about four. There's something about blondes. We treat them differently.

Next to them is Tyler, the giant. Six-foot-three of stupid glued together by testosterone, but you wouldn't want him on the other rugby team, that's for sure. He has muscles

1

upon muscles, and I can't pretend he's not Thor-geous, even if I would rather die than admit it. The last I heard, he was with Scarlett.

Scarlett: the one made of pure evil. Yes, she's beautiful. Yes, she has Pantene-commercial hair falling in perfect chestnut waves over her shoulders. Yes, she has dewy skin, high cheekbones and full lips – but she also has all the warmth of a great white.

Then there's Naima, the vicious one, Seth, the silent smoulderer, with his see-into-my-soul eyes and floppy fringe, and CJ, the little noisy one. There's *always* a little noisy one.

I fantasise about them. They're the stars of my own little made-up drama series in which I'm the lead part. In this recurring daydream, I'm beautiful too, not hideous like I am now, and I stand up to them, lead a rebel alliance. I'd tell them to shut up and die. I'd be with Seth, who I *know* is good underneath it all, and we'd rule benevolently to unite the warring factions of Brecken Heath Academy.

Too late, I realise CJ is looking right at me.

'What are you gawking at, Pizzaface?' I whip my head down, pretending not to hear him. 'She was like, proper staring at you, Ty.'

'She probably fancies you.' I don't need to look up to recognise Scarlett's cyanide voice.

'You-a-want-a-some-pepperoni?' Tyler says in a mock-Italian accent.

On my table, my best friend, Lois, tuts. 'Shall we go, Avery?'

I nod, still not looking up. I hate them so much. Hate is a very strong word, but I mean every drop. As I push my chair back, I knock over my water bottle and its contents gush across the table, trickling over the edge.

The A-List hoot with laughter.

'Nice one, Pizzaface.' This time it's Rufus.

With as much dignity as we can muster, Lois and I exit the canteen, an angry dinner lady calling after us to mop up the water.

We go to the loo to dry off.

'Are you OK?' Lois asks.

Me and Lois have been friends since we started Brecken Heath, back when I wasn't so monstrous. In a parallel world, Lois would probably be one of the A-List – she's so pretty with her Taylor Swift bob and button nose – but, in our unparallel world, she has one 'normal' arm and one funny little arm (her words, not mine). It curls against her chest and she has very little strength in it. The A-List call her 'T-rex'.

'I'm fine.'

Almost as if I want to punish myself for being such a klutz and for making a fool of myself, I look in the mirror. I tilt the hand dryer nozzle up and it blows my hair off my face.

I'm deformed. In the olden days, I'd have belonged in a circus sideshow or scurried the cobbled streets of Victorian London, my face obscured by a veil. Fatima Mahmood doesn't know how lucky she is with her niqab. I've seriously considered getting one.

My chin and cheeks are permanently raging and red – very much like, as Rufus was once quick to point out during physics, the surface of Mars. Lumps and bumps and boils and pustules (that's an especially disgusting word, *pustules*) cover my skin. Some bright red, some pink, some yellow and ripe and ready to burst. Only you can't burst them, because then you'll get scar tissue.

Oh, it's only a few spots. Everyone gets spots. You'll grow out of it.

Well, it's been five years and they don't seem to be getting any better.

And no one warns you about the *pain*. My face *hurts*. All the time, night and day. It feels like there's a needle at the centre of each spot, burrowing down to the bone. I prickle like a cactus. Half the time my skin feels so tight it could rip.

It's hot, it's red, it's angry and so am I. What kind of heinous acts against humanity did I commit in a previous life to wind up like this? It's just not fair. It's not fair that I look like a monster, and it's not fair that Lois was born with a funny little arm.

'You just have to ignore them,' Lois says, fluffing her hair. She really is very pretty, and her mum and dad spoil her rotten with clothes. Not that owning a bit of Burberry will ever elevate her onto the A-List. I'm not being harsh – *they* really are *that* shallow. 'If picking on people's appearances is the best they can do, they're not very imaginative. You know you're fabulous, right, Avery?'

'Oh yeah, I'm the world's undiscovered supermodel.' I roll my eyes at her. 'If only real life came with Photoshop, eh?'

'Rufus and CJ are stupid little boys. It speaks only of their own insecurity that they feel the need to put others down.' She ends her sentence with a little Miss Piggy-style '*humph*'.

I smile. 'Well, I'm not gonna disagree with that. I just really wish that Scarlett Drake could wake up tomorrow with skin like mine.'

You'd be surprised precisely how much time I've frittered away on wishing that.

'Avery! Personally, I'm not going to waste any time on negativity. My grandma always says that all we can do is keep our own front steps clean.'

'What?'

'I *think* she means that all we can do is work on being better people ourselves. I grant you Scarlett looks amazing on the outside, but inside she's as rotten as a mouldy apple.'

I don't say anything, but I can't help but think of PE a few weeks ago when Scarlett kept barrelling a netball at Lois's chest, knowing full well she wouldn't be able to catch it.

Instead I say, 'A mouldy apple with maggots in. And the maggots have leprosy.'

'Yep! Come on, don't let them get you down. We're out of here in a year.'

I think Lois's skin must be thicker than mine. I've lost count of how many times she's brushed off the T-rex thing.

'I know.' I swing my backpack on. 'Come on, let's go and find the others.'

We leave the cafeteria and head for the picnic tables outside the science block. This is where the Year 10 losers hang out, because we know the lab technicians and science teachers will keep an eye out for us. Here we have the music nerds, geeks and general dregs. There are no cute guys, although a lot of the band guys and girls date each other. In fact, it's all quite incestuous, and I find their comings and goings hard to keep up with.

Lois and I sit down with Jess (who, thanks to the A-List, has her very own theme song: *she's big, she's round, she bounces on the ground, it's jumbooooooo Jessica Wright!*) and Viola, who is lovely and very sweet, but who doesn't speak that much English yet because her family only just moved from the Czech Republic. She also wears hearing aids in both ears so it could just be that she can't hear a word we're saying.

Lois and I link up and play a computer game for the rest of lunchtime. Lois manages fine as long as she can rest her DS on the picnic bench. Then when the bell goes we head to registration. I'm so lucky that Lois and I are in the same tutor group.

Unfortunately for both of us, we're also in the same group as Rufus, CJ and Scarlett. They sit at the very back. We sit at the very front. They saunter in at the last possible minute, as ever, so the rest of the class are already seated.

'Thank you for joining us,' says Miss Greenwood, seconds before she starts the register. Miss Greenwood looks about twelve years old. She only qualified last year. She has the frazzled, one-second-away-from-tears air of someone who isn't even close to coping.

'Mozz-a-rella!' Rufus says under his breath as he passes our desk.

'A-spi-cy-meat-a-ball!' adds CJ.

Scarlett says nothing. It's somehow worse.

'Settle down, please,' Miss Greenwood says. 'Scott?'

'Here, Miss.'

'Psst! Avery, do you do stuffed crust?' It's Rufus again. Scarlett laughs and laughs. Some others snigger too. I sink further into my chair.

Miss Greenwood flushes but says nothing, and continues with the register.

Chapter Two

The next day, and every mouthful of Special K turns to putty in my mouth. I struggle to swallow. It's often not so bad once I actually get there, but I've actually started to dread dreading school. I legit worry about worrying.

Mum plonks a glass of Tropicana in front of me. 'Don't forget we have a hospital appointment this afternoon. I'll collect you from the back exit at two-thirty. Don't forget, please!'

I roll my eyes. 'I won't.' Actually, I probably will. 'But maybe you should text me at two just in case?'

Mum smiles. 'What are you like?'

'Not that I see the point in going . . .' I mutter. I decide if I can swallow one more mouthful I can at least claim a victory over breakfast.

'Oh, Avery.' Mum takes a sip of her coffee, then pulls a face. We recently got a Nespresso machine and she's very into trying different pods. 'Don't start all this again . . .'

'I'm not, but if you won't let me have Truisoclear, there's nothing they can do for me, is there?' Even I'm bored of this argument, to be honest. Truisoclear is an acne treatment, but as it also has links to depression and suicidal behaviour, Mum and Dad decided, without my involvement, that I wasn't allowed to go on it. There have been many, many slammed doors over this, but they won't back down.

Dad, I should say, lives three streets away with my stepmum, Julie. It's no biggy, just how it is.

'Avery, you know why.' Mum sits down on the other side of the breakfast table and takes my hand. 'Your skin *will* get better, I promise.'

'What if it doesn't?'

'It will!'

'But what if it *doesn't*?'

I see Mum's eyes glaze over. I don't want to make her cry. 'You are not your skin. It's what's on –'

'It's what's on the inside that counts. Yeah, I've heard that once or twice.' I stand and rinse my bowl out at the sink. 'I'd better go and meet Lois, but I'll see you at two-thirty.' As I leave the kitchen, I can see the pain all over Mum's face.

She should try spending a day wearing mine.

Right after registration, I manage to pick one of my spots by accident. It's a bleeder. After heading for the girls' toilets before assembly, I dab at the wound with some scrunched-up toilet roll. I don't even realise I'm not alone until Lucy Manning, who must have perfected a very stealthy style of weeing, emerges from the end cubicle. I catch her eye for a second in the mirror before I stare into the sink.

'Oh, hi, Avery,' she says in a tone as bright as her blonde. 'How are you?'

Is she kidding? She's alone, thankfully, but that doesn't mean she's not going to scurry back to Scarlett and tell her how she saw me squeezing my acne in the toilets.

'I'm OK,' I mutter.

Lucy washes her hands at the next sink, and there's a deeply awkward silence. Back in primary school, Lucy and I were best friends. Inseparable. Peas in a pod. That was before she ditched me and my deteriorating skin for Scarlett and the A-List as soon as we got to Brecken Heath. I don't look at her, but I can tell she's trying to get my attention.

'So . . .' she says to fill the silence, '. . . have a nice day. I like your bag, by the way. Not my style, but it suits you.'

The thought of My Little Phony Lucy Manning carrying a studded black rubber backpack is almost hilarious. I can't help but smile.

'Thanks.'

'See you around.' Lucy scoops up her Cath Kidston bag and leaves. Two-faced backstabbing witch. At least Scarlett has the decency to act as evil as she seems.

I join Lois in assembly seconds before we have to stand for Mrs Collins, the head of Year 11. What's she doing here? Usually our assemblies are taken by either the head proper or Mr Topping, the head of Year 10. Collins is frankly terrifying, she looks like an evil Russian henchwoman from an action film.

'Good morning, Year 10.'

'GOOOOOD MOOOORNING, MRS COLLINS.'

We sit back down and a gurgle in my tummy warns me that Mrs Collins presence might have something to do with next year's exams. Like any of us need reminding, they test us often enough.

'We have a slightly different assembly today,' she begins. 'It's time to start thinking ahead to next year. As you know, every year, one boy and one girl from Year 11 must represent Brecken Heath Academy as head boy and head girl. We've decided to start the process earlier this year, so the election won't clash with sports day or your end of year exams. To talk to you about what the election entails, here are Dylan and Suriya.'

There's a murmur. Dylan Caldwell and Suriya Kaur are Brecken Heath royalty. Dylan is the first out, gay head boy EVER. He's a semi-famous YouTuber and everything. And Suriya spent last summer helping out in an orphanage in Pakistan. Both make our drab grey uniform look like Prada. They are perfect in every way. I am in awe. I swear they are glowing slightly.

'Good morning, Year 10,' Dylan starts. 'Soon, it'll be time for Suriya and me to leave Brecken Heath.'

'We've loved representing the school, and leading the school council, but it's time for us to pass the baton on to two of you,' Suriya says.

'It's a big responsibility,' Dylan goes on. 'Once a week, you'll meet with the senior leadership team to help give every student at this school a voice.'

'This year, Dylan and I have done everything we can to be that voice and to make this school a better place. We established the Gay/Straight Alliance . . .'

There's a round of applause.

11

'Our Anti-Bullying Week campaign was on the evening news . . .'

'And the canteen now serves gluten-free, dairy-free, vegan and halal options to all pupils.'

More applause.

Dylan becomes more serious for a second. He's so gorgeous. Tyler Oakley once Twitter flirted with him. I saw it.

'We leave this legacy to you, Year 10. Who will continue our good work?'

'It's very simple,' says Suriya, sweeping her mane of velvet-like hair over her shoulder. 'Between now and the end of the month, you can nominate yourself by filling in an application form and placing it in this box.' She gestures to a gaudily painted gold ballot box.

'Once all the nominations are in, we start the campaign,' Dylan says with a grin. 'Candidates will have a month to win over voters before the election on 2nd June. Is that clear?'

An excited buzz fills the hall. Neighbours ask each other if they plan to run. Looking at luminaries like Dylan and Suriya, I guess we must have been a poor intake – there's no one in our whole year who could compare to either of them.

'Who do you think it'll be?' Lois says excitedly.

'I don't know,' I say. 'Could be anyone, I suppose.'

Oh, who am I kidding? It'll be Lucy and Tyler. Of course it will.

It always is.

Chapter Three

Dr Ken Hong's surgery is in a handsome, ivy-covered, red-brick townhouse on the outskirts of the city centre. My dad works for a company that makes braces and retainers (I suppose someone has to) so we get private health care. Not that it's done my face any good.

I'm in the waiting area, leafing through the same issue of *Vogue* that was here at my last appointment six months ago. This shouldn't be allowed: seeing all those flawless models, even though I know they've been airbrushed to within an inch of their lives, isn't making me feel any better about waiting to see a dermatologist.

'Avery Morgan?' The receptionist calls my name. 'Dr Hong is ready now.'

'Be polite, please . . .' Mum breathes in my ear as we enter the office. It's a strange mix of old and new – the room itself is like something from *Downton Abbey*, but the equipment is like something from *Star Trek*.

'Hello there, Avery! Come in and take a seat. How are we?'

They are fine, *I* am disfigured.

'I'm OK.'

'Any change? Let's have a look, shall we?' He steers me to the surgical table thing and I hop on. He shines a blinding lamp in my face and, with latex gloves, pokes and prods my skin. It hurts. I have some big, sore boils on my neck and back too, so he takes a look at them as well. 'And you're still using the face wash?'

'Yes.' I bite my tongue to stop myself from saying it's snake oil.

He makes a non-committal '*hmmm*' noise, and leaves me to get dressed. I join him and Mum at his big mahogany desk. Dr Hong smiles kindly. I've been seeing him for two years now. He's practically family.

'Mrs Morgan, Avery. I know we've discussed this before, but by far the most effective way forward would be for us to discuss medication.'

My heart floats up into my throat like a balloon.

'No.' Mum pops it. 'I'm not having my daughter put at risk. Just no.'

Dr Hong splays his hands like he's surrendering. 'There may be no other alternatives,' he says, looking at his case notes. 'We've tried various methods . . . diet . . . hormones . . . antibiotics . . . but it's quite clear that Avery has chronic *acne vulgaris* and it isn't going to go away by itself. I quite understand why you might have misgivings about Truisoclear – but what if there was something else?'

I look to Mum expectantly, waiting for her response.

'What do you mean?' she says finally.

'I've been invited to find participants to take part in a clinical trial for a new medication . . .'

'A *clinical trial*? No way!' Mum says. 'Avery isn't a guinea pig!'

'Mum . . .' I say, my heart fluttering. New medication? What? The hopeful cortex of my brain suddenly engages.

Dr Hong chuckles. 'No, of course she isn't. Believe me, I'm always sceptical when someone announces a new wonder-drug too, but I've just got back from a conference in San Francisco, and I have to admit that I'm cautiously optimistic about this one.' He hands us both some materials. The brochures are glossy and pastel-coloured. SEBAVECTUM is emblazoned on the front of each one. 'As you can see, the drug is branded as 'Sebavectum'. It's a retinoid compound not unlike Truisoclear, but it has more in common with good old vitamin A, which, of course, you already have in your body. But the vitamin has been paired with a different active ingredient that, in the early trials, doesn't seem to have any of the side-effects often found with the other drugs.'

I've heard promises like this before. The doctor hands them out like lollies at the end of each appointment.

The antibiotics will work. They didn't.

The hormone pills will work. They didn't.

Even so, my eyes tear-up. I can't help it. Hope: it's still there, underneath all the spots and oiliness. Truisoclear without the side-effects . . . It's almost too good to be true.

'Mum? Please?'

'No side-effects?'

Dr Hong shrugs. 'All drugs have some side-effects. You'd expect some dryness of the skin – after all, that's what the medication is meant to be doing – but so far, nothing serious has been reported.'

'How far along are the trials?'

'They're done. It's about to go to market in the States. These trials are just for European standards. Avery would be a perfect candidate. She's stopped growing, and she's unlikely to get pregnant –'

'Too right she is,' Mum chips in.

It's my turn to interrupt. 'It's not one of those trials where I'd be given a placebo, is it?'

That would be worse than no pills at all. I don't think I could get through another car-wreck of disappointment intact.

'Not on this occasion, no. That stage of testing is finished.'

I look at the girl on the front of the brochure, laughing gormlessly at a bottle of mineral water. Great skin though.

'Mum? Can I?'

She inhales deeply. 'Oh, I don't know, Avery, I mean . . .'

'Mum, *please*. He said there's no side effects; what have we got to lose?'

She squeezes my hand tight. 'You, Avery! I have you to lose.'

'Please . . .' I start to cry. Stupid weak tear ducts. 'I can't go on like this, Mum. I just can't. Please . . .'

Yeah, I'm begging. What of it?

Dr Hong hands me a tissue and I bury my face in it. I often find that once I start, I've unclogged a dam and I can't stop. Now I can't breathe for tears, and where there are tears there is snot.

'OK,' Mum says, although I hardly hear her. 'But I'm not promising anything before I speak to your dad.'

'Really?' Dad is a soft-touch: if Mum's on-board, it's in the bag. 'You mean it?' I dry my eyes.

'I promise we'll talk about it.' She looks Dr Hong firmly in the eye. 'I'm sorry, but I'm going to want a second opinion, and I want to do some research of my own as well.'

'Completely understandable. Take as much time as you need.'

There's a 'before-and-after' photo of a patient in the brochure – a guy about my age with perhaps even worse acne than mine in his 'before' picture. In the 'after' picture though, his skin is California-gold and blemish free.

'It really works?' I ask.

'I've seen it with my own eyes,' Dr Hong says. 'I can even send you videos. In the medical profession, we don't use words like "miracle cure", because it's not a miracle. It's simply good, old-fashioned science.'

I look again at the before-and-after guy.

I need this drug in my life.

As soon as we've had dinner, which tonight was KFC (it's a post-dermatologist cheer-me-up ritual) I head over to Lois's. Lois lives in a much nicer house than mine, opposite the park. There's a high wall running around the house, and the pond in her back garden is big enough to have ducks living in it. The only downside is that she also only lives three houses away from Scarlett Drake. You can smell the evil wafting over from her garden.

In her bedroom (which is considerably larger than even my Mum's), I bounce up and down on Lois's bed while she reads the brochure from the clinic.

'Oh my god, Ave, this is amazing! Do you think they'll let you?'

I flop down onto my bum and roll to the edge of the bed.

'I think so. I forced Mum to go round to Dad's *tonight*. I said I'd go on hunger strike if she didn't, which would have been hard because of, hello, Zinger Tower Burger.'

Lois laughs. 'Oh, I really hope they let you. If it works like it says it works, you'd see results in two weeks! How amazing would that be?'

I grimace. 'I was such a hot mess. I cried like a baby. I think she'll cave.'

I lie back and look up at the ceiling.

Lois closes the brochure and lies alongside me. 'Good! You deserve this, Avery, you've suffered long enough. It's just a shame there's not a pill for my arm, really.'

I suddenly feel like a total moron for bleating on about my wonder-cure.

'Lois . . . that's not what I meant . . . I . . . we shouldn't have to change for anyone . . . it's just . . . my skin is . . . *so* . . .'

She turns to me and smiles. 'That's not what I meant either! I'm excited for you! You're already beautiful because of your radiant inner specialness, but if this is something you need, then I got your back, bae. I'm your ride-or-die!'

I will NOT cry again. I blink back the tears.

'I really do. I need these pills.'

I close my eyes and make a wish – no, more than a wish, a prayer. *If Mum lets me do this, I'll do* anything. I engrave a promise onto the universe. *I'll be better, I'll be the best I can be.*

18

Chapter Four

Exactly one week later, I'm standing in front of the bathroom mirror. I pop my first Sebavectum out of the blister pack. It's a tiny powder-pink pill. It's funny how something so small can feel so huge. This is momentous. So much expectation in one little pill – you'd think it'd weigh more.

Dad, as expected, said he'd support whatever Mum decided. Mum then sat me down and warned me that if I so much as felt drowsy, she'd stop the trial, and, reluctantly, I agreed to her terms. Dr Hong himself was only too happy to enrol me on the program.

So, bottoms up!

I throw the pill to the back of my mouth and take a big gulp of water.

Done.

And now all I can do is wait. I look at my reflection and scrape my hair off my face. I don't know what I'm expecting – perhaps some sort of instantaneous reaction where my diseased skin peels off like a satsuma to reveal a flawless complexion beneath.

Shame, that'd be cool. But kinda gross.

I can't imagine my life without the spots. I've never seen my teenage face without them. Well, now's not the time to get nostalgic. These little parasites have lived on me for long enough. Sayonara, ladies!

I flick out the light.

The next morning, when my alarm goes off, I've never jumped out of bed faster – even on Christmas Day. I run to the bathroom and tug the light on, ready to see if there's been an overnight miracle.

There hasn't.

I knew there wouldn't be really, but it's still a bit of an anticlimax.

I have to keep a diary as part of the trial. It's an official form thing that Dr Hong gave me. I figure if I fill it in each morning before breakfast, I won't forget.

DAY 1: No change. No side-effects.

I go to school. It's the same as every other day except Mrs Garner is off sick, so instead of PE we get to hang out and draw pictures in one of the science labs. No one complains.

DAY 2: No change.

DAY 3: No change, and in RE CJ asks me, 'Why don't you just wash your face more often?' Ah, that old chestnut. On the plus side, it's the last day before half-term.

DAY 4: I don't know if I'd call it a change, but my lips are super-dry. It's nothing a little Vaseline won't fix, but it's the first sign that change is afoot. Come on, Sebavectum, do your worst.

My skin is still horrific. It's a Saturday, so Dad takes me to see the new Marvel film and we have pizza afterwards. Yes, despite everything, pizza is still delicious to me. We have a half-and-half Hawaiian/Meat Feast.

DAYS 5, 6, 7: Lips still a little sore. Sounds a bit hideous, but skin feels *drier*, less oily somehow.

I take a selfie and I'm decidedly less shiny than normal. Some of the older spots are peeling a bit. I can't decide if I'm imagining it, but my face feels less painful too. Fingers crossed.

DAY 8: I'm *not* imagining it. Today, for the first time, I can see a real difference. My skin looks loads less red and far less angry. Sebavectum is supposed to prevent new spots *and* claims to speed up the healing of old ones too. It's taken over a week, but I think we're getting somewhere.

Lois has gone to Cornwall with her parents but this is so exciting I give her a call to tell her.

DAYS 9, 10: Skin is now quite dry, so I moisturise as directed. When I touch it, my skin doesn't hurt any more. Even this is reason enough to have a marching-band parade down the high street. It's still not perfect, but it's SO MUCH BETTER.

DAYS 11, 12: It's Sunday and tomorrow we go back to school. Back in front of the mirror after my bath, I pull my hair into a knot on top of my head. I can hardly believe it. For the first time in three years I have more face than spots. I look human. Sure, there are still gentle, salmon-pink marks, but my skin is smoother, clearer, whiter than I can remember it being in forever. My face is healing.

I cry. I sit down cross-legged on the bath mat and have a lovely little cry.

Chapter Five

'I can't believe it!' Lois says as we walk to school through the park. 'I can't believe how much it's improved in a week!'

'A week and a half, but who's counting?'

For the first time in living memory, I've tied my hair back into a messy Katniss/Queen Elsa plait. There hasn't exactly been an inspirational makeover moment, but it feels good to not have to hide my face. Right now, my skin – although not perfect *yet* – doesn't look that much worse than anyone else's. It sounds stupid, but *looking up* – not staring down at the pavement – makes it a whole new journey into school. I see blossom swirling down from the trees like confetti, red-faced joggers with swishy ponytails, and dog-walkers struggling with bundles of pugs and French bulldogs.

'Do you think people will say stuff?' Lois asks, almost giddy.

'I doubt anyone will even notice, to be honest.'

But they do.

As ever, we head for the picnic tables outside the science block. Right away, Viola compliments my hair while Jessica Wright says, 'Don't take this the wrong way, Avery, but your skin is looking really good.' A couple of the other people from the maths and science crew agree.

I just smile and say, 'Thank you,' although I'm beaming inside.

At morning break, Christian Dudley, a guy who hangs out with us, stops me at the water fountain.

'Hi, Avery.' He lowers his voice. 'I know this is like, totally none of my business, but are you using Truisoclear for your skin? It's just that I think I'm going to try it too. Is it OK?'

I don't really need the whole school knowing I'm on meds, but Christian's forehead acne is pretty bad, and I did make a pledge to the universe to be nicer . . . 'Actually, no. I'm on a drug trial for something new called Sebavectum. My doctor gave it to me.'

'Oh yeah, I think I've read about it online. Looks like it's working . . . ?'

'Yeah, seems to be.'

'Cool! Thanks, Avery.'

Of course this was a huge mistake. By lunchtime, Lois told me she'd been informed by Carrie Holley that I was on a miracle-cure drug trial. Word travels fast.

'God, how bored must people be if they're talking about my skin? Didn't anyone get murdered, or worse – knocked-up – over the holidays?'

'Oh, it doesn't matter,' Lois assures me. 'People have eyes! I doubt anyone would have thought your skin just changed like it was the immaculate complexion or something!'

I laugh but I'm bugged. 'They might have. People do just grow out of it.'

'Well, maybe now you can be a role model for other kids with bad skin.'

I hadn't thought of that. 'This is true.'

Next period is maths, which I hate because Lois is in the set higher than me and so I have to sit without her. Instead I sit with Viola on the front row nearest the door and wait for Mr Parker to arrive. Everyone knows he chain-smokes up to three cigarettes before a lesson, so he's always late.

I'm reading my book, a well-loved copy of *Bonjour Tristesse*, when I realise there's a shadow looming over me. It's Lucy Manning.

'Hi, Avery! Everyone's talking about your skin!'

'Um . . . OK.'

'No, not like that! Everyone's saying how much better is it.' She smiles warmly and I can't help but smile back. 'You look amazing! You must be so thrilled.'

'Er, yeah, I guess it's better.'

'You really deserve this, Avery.'

I swear the room temperature drops about twelve degrees as Scarlett and Naima sweep into the room and stand alongside Lucy. Lucy's eyes dip as if she's been caught talking to someone she shouldn't.

'Oh, wow, so it's true.' Scarlett scrutinises my face.

I say nothing. My tongue goes on strike.

With a manicured hand, Scarlett actually reaches out and tilts my chin upwards.

'Good cheekbones, babes,' she says. 'Who knew?'

And then she smiles a perfect smile. I want to tell her to let go of my face. I want to tell her I hate her. I want to tell her there's no little pink pill to clear up her tar-black soul.

But on the other hand, Scarlett Drake thinks I have nice cheekbones, and coming from her that means more than it would from any other girl in the school.

I feel pretty.

I smile back.

Chapter Six

The next couple of weeks fly by. I spring out of bed as my alarm happily chimes, and every morning my skin seems just that little bit smoother and clearer. A pleasing side-effect of the drugs is that my hair has become newsreader-huge – I don't know if the meds are drying it out or something, but it's never looked thicker or shinier.

At school, people are falling over themselves to find out about Sebavectum. I guess, as the epicentre of acne at Brecken Heath, I didn't really *see* that anyone else had spots, but apparently plenty of people do, and they all want to know where I got the medication from.

A group of Year 9 girls gather around me. 'Seriously,' I say, relishing their adoring glances, 'after the first week, I'd already started seeing results. You should get your parents to talk to Dr Hong.'

A couple of them jot the name down.

'Avery, you look so pretty!' says a little girl I swear I've never met.

'Thank you!'

Even teachers have quietly taken me to one side and told me how pleased they are that my ordeal is over.

Of course I'm loving it, although I have now started having a recurring dream where I wake up one morning and find that my skin has reverted to its former state. I always wake with a start and my hands fly to my cheeks to check they're still clear.

When you only have one proper friend, the worst thing in the world is when that friend is off sick. It's day twenty-four of the trial and Lois has the flu, so I'm all alone. The day drags. In the afternoon I have double biology and sit by myself near the front.

There is some excitement when Mrs Walsh enters wearing a white coat, which means we're doing something practical instead of merely going through old exam papers. My excitement quickly dies when she says, 'Can you get yourself into pairs, please?'

Oh god no. I look around and everyone else is already sitting in pairs. I can feel panic rising – what if I have to join a three with Scarlett or something?

There's a tap on my shoulder. It's Lucy.

'Hi! Rufus is off sick, wanna be my partner?'

Well, this is surreal. I look to the back row and see Scarlett paired with Tyler. She's obviously given Lucy permission to join me.

'Yeah, sure.'

'Thanks.' Lucy hops onto the stool next to mine. She smells of the DKNY perfume that's a bit like apples. 'I didn't want to get stuck with Matthew Pinder. He'd just stare at my chest for the next two hours.'

'No worries.' I smile awkwardly.

28

Mrs Walsh describes the practical. It's pretty straightforward stuff. We're comparing the vitamin C content of various fruit juices using a chemical called DCPIP – shouldn't be too hard. We potter about, getting all the test tubes and pipettes and samples we need. Before we start we have to copy out a results table.

Suddenly Lucy says, 'Do you remember our detective agency?'

'Oh, wow!' I put my pen down. 'That is so cringe, I haven't thought about that in years! What was it called again?'

'The Jade Dolphin Detective Agency!'

I laugh. 'Because you're favourite colour was jade . . .'

'And dolphins were your favourite animal!'

'On reflection,' I say, 'it kinda sounds like a brothel in Chinatown.'

Now Lucy laughs, freely and throatily, the way we used to. 'To be fair, we did solve a fairly massive mystery.'

'My grandma did indeed learn who had smashed her ornamental china rose. I don't think my cousin Nick has ever quite forgiven me for ratting him out.'

Lucy pouts. 'It's a shame we stopped hanging out. I miss you sometimes.'

I wonder if I'm keeping the gobsmackedness off my face. I'm not the one who traded-up the instant we got to secondary school.

I shrug. 'One of those things.'

'We used to have so much fun though! Don't you think?'

Her smile is so sweet and honest, I can't help but wonder if she even knows the harm she does. Just by *being* she makes the rest of us feel terrible about ourselves. I don't suppose she can help her fortune in the biological lottery, but like it or not, Lucy Manning is the standard by which the rest of us are judged.

'We did,' I concede. 'I miss you too, but . . . things have changed.'

'Well, they can change back! We're not eleven any more, there's no reason we can't all be friends.'

That earns a mighty eye-roll. 'Oh yeah, like that's gonna happen.'

'What? Scarlett? She's a pussycat! Come on, let's go and work over there.'

My heart almost cracks my ribs.

'Lucy, no!'

Too late. Lucy has already swept up our rack of test tubes and is heading to the back of the lab.

'We're gonna work here!' Lucy announces.

'This is so stupid,' Scarlett laments. 'When am I ever going to need to know how much vitamin C there is in orange juice? Do you ever just feel like you're just totally wasting your time in a state-sanctioned holding pen?'

'Scarlett.' Lucy ignores her. 'You know Avery, right?'

'Sure. How's it going?'

How can such a simple question be so hard to answer? I can't work out if it's a trick designed to make me look stupid somehow. When has she ever asked me how it's going before?

'Yeah, I'm fine.'

'Awesome. Do you actually know what we have to do?'

'Vaguely . . .'

'That'll do. I was playing Candy Crush while Walsh was droning on. Someone wants to tell her that when there's that much vodka in her orange juice, the vitamin C content hardly matters.' (There are certain *rumours* about Mrs Walsh . . .)

'Come on,' Lucy steps in. 'It's easy. I'll show you.'

We follow the method closely, speaking only about the experiment. Scarlett is, dare I say it, friendly. I see other people looking over, and why wouldn't they? It's today's episode of *The A-List*, and I'm making a cameo.

Results recorded, I take our test tubes to the sink to be rinsed. I loiter behind Tyler and Seth while they wash up.

'. . . I dunno, maybe,' says Seth.

'She seeing anyone?' Tyler hands him some pipettes.

'Don't think so, but is it a bit weird?'

'Dunno,' Tyler shrugs his huge shoulders.

'I guess I never really saw her before, but she's gorgeous.'

'Nah. Her skin's better, but she still dresses like a dude.'

With horror, I realise that they're talking about me. Oh, this is awkward but . . . did Seth Curran just call me gorgeous? I start to skulk silently away.

'Tyler, you sexist pig!' I turn around and find Scarlett standing right behind me. '"Dresses like a dude"? What would you like her to wear? A bikini?'

Tyler and Seth turn, caught red-handed. Seth's face turns milk-white.

'Were you standing there the whole time?'

'Yep, and it was very rude of you to objectify poor Avery.'

They stand before Scarlett like guilty little boys who've smashed a greenhouse window. OK. I've seen Scarlett's

31

Instagram and she's more than happy to be objectified – more often than not she's just a pair of dismembered bare legs – so her little diatribe is purely about letting Tyler know who's in charge. Hierarchy-wise, I see now that Scarlett is the queen of the boys too – the supremest-being among the supreme.

'Sorry, Avery,' Tyler mutters. 'Your clothes are . . . nice.'

With Scarlett at my side, I feel brave and take a risk.

'That's OK, Tyler. I can get new clothes at the shops, but there's not a lot we do about your face, is there?' I say with a smile.

Both Scarlett and Seth crack up, as even Tyler has to submit to 'the bants'.

'Oh, snap!' Scarlett says. 'You deserved that too! Here . . .' she takes the test tubes out of my hand and gives them to Tyler. 'He can wash up as punishment.'

Scarlett hooks her arm around mine, and we walk back to the table. But Seth follows us, and gently pulls me to one side.

'Avery, I'm so sorry, that's properly embarrassing. I didn't know you were there, honest.'

'Clearly.'

'Uh, cringe. I don't know if this saves it, but I meant it. You look awesome . . . and not just your skin, although obviously that's amazing. I'm babbling. Man! What I mean is, you seem . . . different all over. Sorry, I'm no good at compliments!'

I feel my cheeks burn. 'Well, thank you, Seth.' I don't know what else to say, so I busy myself sweeping things into my rucksack. The funny thing is though, I do *feel* different all over. It's like the Sebavectum has changed my face *and* my brain.

As the lesson ends, people frantically snatch the homework assignment off Mrs Walsh's desk and make a run for the door. But three girls block my path: Scarlett, Lucy and Naima.

'Are you doing anything Friday night?' Scarlett asks.

'Erm . . . why?'

'My parents are going to this ludicrous wine tasting thing, so we're having a pizza and DVD night at mine if you wanna come?'

'Are you serious?'

Scarlett smiles. 'Of course I am. Avery, you're like a beautiful-if-slightly-awkward caterpillar emerging from a chrysalis. Own it. You could totally be one of the hottest girls in the year. Whether you like it or not, your stock is about to skyrocket and you're going to need people who know what they're talking about to help you play the market. And let's face it, we girls gotta stick together.'

I'm still waiting for the punchline. This girl has called me Pizzaface for three years. Naima once coloured in a sanitary towel with red marker and stuck it to my back. I walked around with it attached to me for about an hour before a teacher rescued me.

'I dunno . . .'

'Come on! It's *Pitch Perfect* and ice cream! What is there to think about?' It's as if the last three years have never happened. 'And we can talk about you and Seth . . .'

Chapter Seven

'What am I supposed to do?'

After school I go straight over to Lois's. It transpires she doesn't have the flu, she has a cold, and will probably be back at school tomorrow. She's on the sofa watching *Friends*, surrounded by screwed-up tissues and mugs of half-finished Lemsip.

'OMG! This is amazing! You have to go! You can spy on her and find out all her dirt so we can bring her down!'

I sit at a microbe-safe distance, pulling my legs under me and onto the armchair. 'I dunno. I keep thinking it's all a trick and Scarlett's gonna do something awful to me, you know like that thing with your hand in a bucket of water to make you wee yourself.'

'That's not Scarlett's style. She'd get Naima to do it.' Lois blows her nose. 'I can't believe how shallow she really is. She's been nothing but horrid to us and now you're a minor celebrity she's inviting you over for a slumber party!'

I haven't told Lois the only reason I'm even considering accepting the invite is the vague possibility of a date with Seth. I don't know what Lois would think about that. I mean, Seth has never directly said anything mean to me or Lois, but he does hang around with the very worst people in the world.

'It's so weird being around them. It's like people off the TV have crawled into the real world, like that girl from *The Ring*. What do Scarlett, Lucy and Naima talk about in private? I dread to think.'

'Ten bucks says it's nothing but boys and make up.'

'Oh, come on, what do we ever talk about? Nuclear fission?'

Lois laugh-coughs. 'Valid point. Actually we mostly talk about *them*, so you have to go. It'll be awful, though.'

'Well, *obviously*.'

'Just don't you dare dump me for Scarlett Drake . . .'

I roll my eyes. 'Oh, as if! This whole thing is a huge mistake. I must be mad.'

'But you'll go?'

I think my mind is made up. I do want to go. I can't not.

I'm so overdressed. I spent hours labouring over what to wear to Scarlett's house, in the end choosing a denim skirt and flannel shirt. But it turns out I needn't have bothered. Scarlett welcomes me into her grand hallway wearing sweatpants and a vest.

'Hi, Avery, come on in. We're in the snug.'

Scarlett's home is beautiful, and just how I always imagined: white, pristine and like something from *Real Housewives*. Crystal chandeliers hang from the ceiling and creamy roses spill from vases.

It's like being in a doll's house.

I follow Scarlett into a lounge with fat sofas and the biggest flatscreen TV I've ever seen. Naima and Lucy are already here, as dressed-down as Scarlett is.

'Perfect timing!' Lucy says. 'The pizza just arrived.'

'Oh, awesome.' Boots removed, I join them in kneeling around a coffee table.

'Diet Coke?' Naima offers, still eyeing me up slightly.

'Please.' I notice there's only one medium-sized pizza on the coffee table. 'Is there more?'

Scarlett looks at me warily. 'Is there something wrong with this one?'

It's only two slices each, but I know better than to challenge her.

'No, it's great.'

'It's such a treat,' Scarlett says. 'We try not to eat bread.'

'We don't eat at all at school,' Lucy says, somewhat grumpily.

'What?' I ask in mild horror.

Scarlett sighs as if she's bored of having to endlessly recite the same rules. 'Eating looks disgusting. If there was a pretty way to eat, I'd do it. When people eat they look like animals, and how is that attractive?'

I'm suddenly very aware that I've just shoved a huge wedge of pizza into my mouth.

'Are you for real?'

'I'm deadly serious.'

'Are boys allowed to eat in public?'

'Boys don't need to look pretty, do they?' Scarlett says defiantly. 'It's about having a little self-control. I'm not saying don't eat – boys don't like bony girls . . .'

36

'Like Esme Peterson,' Naima says, casually picking a mushroom off the pizza. Esme is a very anorexic girl in the year above us.

'. . . I'm just saying maintain an air of feminine mystery. If you have to eat in public because you are, for example, on a picnic with a boy, then eat small finger foods that don't need much chewing.'

'Like a grape,' Lucy offers helpfully. Her training must have taken.

'It's common sense. Anyone can be gorgeous. It just takes hard work and self-discipline.'

'Otherwise,' Naima says with a grin, 'you end up like that fat beast Jessica Wright.'

I almost choke on my pizza.

'God,' Scarlett says, suddenly wide-eyed. 'How can she have let herself get like that? I blame the parents. She should have been taken into care as a child.'

Lucy tuts. 'Scarlett, don't be . . .'

'Don't be what?' Scarlett discards the one slice of pizza that she's half-eaten. 'Mean? I'm not, Luce, I'm being *honest*. Are you denying that Jessica Wright weighs roughly the same as a minibus full of baby hippos? Avery.' She turns to me. 'Do you think I'm evil?'

Dear Earth, please swallow me up.

'Erm . . . minibus? That's kinda harsh.' *Kinda harsh*? I am a coward. A terrible coward.

'I'm the voice of the big, bad world, Avery. Ain't nobody got time for *nice*, and if you think that pretending Jessica Wright isn't a mammoth is doing her a favour, you're crazy.

37

If a teacher at primary school had told Jessica to drop about ten stone, *that* would've be the kinder thing to have done. I mean, what hope does she have? Honestly? She's doomed.' Scarlett pauses to sip her Diet Coke elegantly through a straw. 'Here's a scenario for you: if Lucy and Jessica turned up to work at your . . . let's say *restaurant*, as a hostess, which would you employ? *Honestly*.'

All three girls look at me, and I feel like one of those divers in a shark cage.

'I guess . . . Lucy?'

'Of course you would,' Scarlett says triumphantly. 'Because who's gonna wanna eat watching lint collect in Jessica's back-rolls? And it's the same thing with your skin. Now you're gorgeous, the world is your oyster. Seriously, I figured out, like, when I was about six, that you get special treatment when you're pretty. Work it, babes. Facts of life.'

The problem is, her voice has also been the little voice in my head for a long, long time.

I *hate* her, but I agree with her, and now I hate myself.

She's cruel.

She's a monster.

She must be stopped.

Coming here was a terrible mistake.

'I'm not gorgeous,' I mutter.

'You will be after I've finished with you.'

'What?'

Scarlett shares a sly smile with Lucy and Naima. 'We have a little surprise for you . . . Tyler and Seth are coming over at nine!'

38

I almost hurl the pizza right back up. How 'pretty' would that be?

'For real?'

'I wouldn't lie, babes. As soon as Seth knew you were coming over, he asked if he could come too. So, we need to get you ready . . .'

'Makeover!' Lucy declares, clapping her hands.

'Avery Morgan.' Scarlett smiles. 'Welcome to the A-List.'

Chapter Eight

In literary terms, 'uncanny', derives from the German phrase *Das Unheimliche*, and translates as 'the opposite of what is familiar', or, in other words, a strange and peculiar mixture of the familiar and unfamiliar.

Sitting in front of the mirror at Scarlett Drake's dresser, 'uncanny' hardly did the weirdness justice.

While Scarlett worked on my face and Lucy fixed my eyebrows, Naima took curling irons to my hair, each lock sizzling and steaming, and then falling into relaxed ringlets. Now she instructs me to bend over, shake it out and toss it back. I sit back down and look at the finished effect.

OH MY . . .

I look like me but not me.

Now, I've always avoided make up like the plague as I was convinced it would make my skin worse. But with a little, Scarlett has created a lot. She's totally transformed my face. This doppelganger's eyes are framed with black kohl and smoky eye shadow. Foundation covers any final pink acne marks; subtle blusher brings out my cheekbones; powder has been brushed over my skin to make my forehead less shiny, and a frankly delicious raspberry lip gloss seems to have plumped my lips to anaphylactic proportions.

I look like Scarlett. This wasn't a makeover, it was a Drakeover. I'm her clone and it's too scary for words.

'There, look at you all grown-up. And just in time too. It's five to nine.'

'You like?' Lucy asks.

'I . . . I don't look like me.'

'Thank god,' Naima says, before adding, 'Joking, babes!'

Scarlett scrutinises me. 'Who is it you look like?'

Erm . . . you?

'I don't know . . .'

'I know who it is! That girl from the film with that guy in!'

'Oh, *her*.'

'You know who I mean! She's gorgeous, and so are you.' Downstairs, the doorbell chimes. 'That's the guys! You ready?'

'Not really . . .'

'It'll be fine.' Scarlett pulls off her pyjamas and slips into some spray-on jeans and an even tighter vest top. 'Come on.'

Lucy takes my hand as I give myself a final check in the full-length mirror on the wardrobe. I look a bit reality TV to be honest, but too late to change now.

'Don't worry,' Lucy tells me. 'Seth is a decent guy.'

I don't really know how to put the cavalcade of worries I'm currently experiencing into English. I don't even know where to begin.

'I'm nervous.' Seems like a good place to start.

Lucy drags me over the landing towards the stairs. 'Don't

41

be.' She leans in closer and whispers in my ear. 'And if it gets too crazy, just give me a shout and I'll come and rescue you. I promise.'

I can tell that she means it, and I feel about forty per cent better. I suddenly feel a little guilty for the hours I've spent calling Lucy every prostitute-related name under the sun . . . And to think I call myself a feminist. I still don't understand why she hangs around with the other two, though.

Booming, deep, male voices rattle up the stairs. Ugh, they've brought Rufus and CJ too. Well, of course they have. Lucy and I trot down the last few stairs and I feel like a debutante at the Evil Debutante's Ball.

The guys fall silent and I realise I'm the reason why. I stop them dead in their tracks. I'm a conversation killer. Their eyes scan me over. I must look like I'm about to audition for *RuPaul's Drag Race*. I'm so embarrassed.

'Oh, wow,' Rufus starts but Lucy silences him with a gentle slap to his chest.

'Stop staring,' I mutter.

Seth snaps out of it first. 'Sorry, you look amazing!'

Amazing? Is he kidding?

'It took me a minute to work out who it was.' He smiles warmly. 'Is Avery under there somewhere?'

I smile back.

'Great job on the makeover, Scarlett,' CJ says. 'You look bang-tidy, Avery.'

'She looks like you.' Big dumb Tyler states the obvious.

Scarlett stands by my side like she's presenting me as her show-and-tell project. 'We could be sisters, right?'

'I don't know which sister I'd rather . . .' CJ begins before Scarlett's frosty glare silences him. She and I both know I'll never be hotter than Scarlett, firstly because she'll never allow it, and secondly because I don't know how to do that walk she does. The one where she thrusts her chest forward and bum back simultaneously. If I do that I look like a pigeon.

'So let's get the party started!' Scarlett says. 'My dad won't notice if we steal a little tipple from his drinks cabinet. Seth, you know where it is, right?'

'The mini-bar in the study?'

'Sure! Avery, why don't you go and help him choose something? But don't steal too much or my dad will kill me.' Scarlett practically pushes me into Seth's arms.

The others peel off into the snug and I follow Seth down the hall.

'That was subtle,' he says quietly.

'Like a steamhammer.' *What?* 'I mean sledgehammer. Or steamroller.'

He laughs and my shoulders unclench a little.

'So you let Scarlett dress you up?'

'Not quite.' I have to fight the urge to hide behind my hair. Old habits. 'The clothes are mine, but yeah, I got an inspirational makeover moment.'

The door to the study creaks as Seth slips inside. He flicks on the light and I see we're in a proper, oak-panelled study. It smells of cigars and money.

'You don't have to do everything Scarlett says, you know.'

'I don't intend to. I'm just a tourist. Seeing how the other half live.'

Seth tousles his hair. 'I know, right? Look at all this stuff. And you wanna see Naima's house, it's double the size of this place again.'

I notice that the whole of one wall is devoted to the trophies and certificates the Drake family have accumulated. 'Are all these Scarlett's?'

'Some of them. She's got two sisters and a brother.'

Accomplished ones at that. The eldest sister seems to be a doctor, like her father. The brother appears to be some sort of pro rugby player, and Scarlett's other sister has just won an award at the Cambridge University debate society. Quite the family of overachievers.

Seth is busy at the mini-bar, rummaging around half-finished bottles. 'Any requests?'

'None for me, thanks.'

'Cool.'

I'm glad he doesn't push it. The absolute last thing I need is to get drunk and make a fool of myself.

'What about you?' I change the subject. 'You don't live in a mansion?'

'Are you kidding?' He swipes an old bottle of Kahlua that looks like it's been there since the eighties. 'After Dad died, Mum decided to sell the old place. We live in the Old Mill apartments by the river.'

What? With the amount of time I've spent staring at Seth Curran, how did I not know his dad had died?

'Oh. I'm sorry.'

He shrugs it off, but I can tell his brevity is hiding something. 'It's OK. He was really sick. I know it's a cliché to say it's a relief when an ill person dies, but it kind of was. Does that make me sound awful?'

The sound of the grandfather clock ricochets off the wooden walls, counting out awkward seconds.

'Erm . . . no.' I don't know what to say. 'Do you want to talk about it?'

Seth comes close and places a hand on my bare arm. At the touch of his skin, colours suddenly become more colourful. My chest feels hotter.

'I really don't, but you're the first person in a long time who's offered to listen.'

We're in a MOMENT. I can feel it. I almost drift up out of my body and watch us like we're in a soap: neatly framed profiles, face-to-face. I never, ever thought I'd get a *moment*. But I have, and it's with Seth.

Is this where we kiss? Am I about to get a kiss?

No. Naima barges through the door.

'What are you doing? We're thirsty!'

The air changes in an instant and Seth holds out the Kahlua.

'Will this do?'

Uh. Kiss fail. Epic kiss fail.

Chapter Nine

The debrief is at Lois's the next morning.

'So did you sacrifice something to Satan? Does she have a burn book? Is she really a . . . a lizard person?'

'A lizard person?'

'I dunno. What happened?'

We're sat in Lois's back garden and I'm very aware that Scarlett is but three fences away.

'Nothing. They got tipsy on Kahlua and watched YouTube videos of people falling off things.'

Lois blinks. 'That's it?'

'Yep.'

I decide against telling her about the MOMENT with Seth. I don't know why, she'd be thrilled, but it just makes me seem so shallow, like all of a sudden I'm totally preoccupied with thoughts of a boy. Or, more specifically, his lips.

I spent all last night wide-awake, fantasising about what the kiss would have been like. The MOMENT has changed to a panoramic cliff-top, complete with Hollywood rain and a violin crescendo. Does it make me a terrible person to want a kiss? Answer: yes, if it means sucking up to Scarlett Drake.

'I'm almost disappointed that she didn't do anything evil.'

'I wouldn't go that far. You missed her diatribe about why overweight people are doomed. It was all very Katie Hopkins.'

'Did she say anything about me?' Lois grimaces.

'No. I swear.'

'That witch. I'm not even relevant enough to talk about.'

I laugh out loud and throw a Scarlett-sanctioned grape at her head.

Monday starts, as ever, with assembly. Once again we're joined by Kapitán Collins so I guess we're discussing the upcoming election.

'Good morning Year 10.'

'GOOOOOOD MOOOOORNING, MRS COLLINS.'

'Mr Topping is actually taking assembly this morning, but I wanted to remind you that this is the last week to nominate yourself for the head boy and head girl election. I must say, Year 10, the response has been somewhat underwhelming. So far only the following people have put themselves forward . . .'

There's a mumblation as people start to speculate.

'That was *not* an invitation to start talking. So far for the boys, we have Tyler Broomfield, Seth Curran, Rufus Shelton and Stewart Parris.'

Interesting. Tyler I expected, and Rufus I understand, but I wouldn't have thought it'd be Seth's thing. Stewart Parris is the Year 10 store's-own brand version of Dylan Caldwell. It's one thing to be out-and-proud, it's another to be an obnoxious, two-faced gossip. He holds sway in the theatre group, but otherwise doesn't stand a chance.

'And for the girls, it's even worse. So far only Maddy French, Alice Deevers and Scarlett Drake have put themselves forward.'

As Mrs Collins goes on, my heart sinks. Scarlett's got it in the bag. Maddy French is the netball captain so will probably drum up some support from the sporty girls, but no one else. Alice 'The Beaver' Deevers (on account of her prominent teeth – nothing rude) is an almost sociopathically righteous do-gooder. There's no one she hasn't alienated in her fervent quest for 'social justice'. Literally only Alice will vote for Alice.

This is so bad. Scarlett as head girl? I think about all the horrible things she said about Jessica, the time she told her friends she couldn't eat while looking at my face, the countless times she's hummed the *Jurassic Park* theme in earshot of Lois. Bestowing a title on her somehow validates her, makes it all legitimate. It makes me feel nauseous.

'Are you OK?' Lois asks me.

'No. This is the actual very worst.'

Mrs Collins is still talking. 'Oh, come on, Brecken Heath! Where's your school spirit? If nothing else, just think how wonderful this will look on your university applications. You have until the end of the week to get your name in the ballot box. Please consider it.'

The next lesson is maths and I take the opportunity to grab Lucy.

'Aren't you going for head girl?' Realistically I know Lucy is the only serious contender who could dethrone Scarlett.

'Are you kidding? Scarlett would skin me alive.'

I fight the urge to shake her by the shoulders. 'Really? I think she can handle some competition.' This is a lie, but I'm getting desperate. Seeing Scarlett lose would be too exquisite.

Lucy scrunches her pretty nose. 'No way. It's a major deal for her. You know, like, her sisters and brother were all head boy or head girl.'

'You shouldn't be scared of her – you're best friends! She'd understand if you wanted to go for it, I'm sure.'

'I'm not *scared* of her,' Lucy says so defensively she has to be. 'It's just more hassle than it's worth. If you're that bothered, why aren't you going for it?'

I snort in a very un-pretty manner. 'Are you kidding?'

'Well, why not?'

For about seven thousand reasons, the first of which being that I'm *definitely* scared of Scarlett. Right on cue, she struts in, clutching Tyler's arm.

'How cool is this?' she purrs. 'Head boy and head girl!'

The knife twists between my ribs.

I'm becoming pretty certain that most business happens over toilet sinks, and not in boardrooms. Case in point: I'm washing my hands when I realise reigning head girl Suriya Kaur is standing right next to me.

'Hey, you're Avery Morgan, right?'

'Yeah.'

'Nice to meet you. I'm Suriya.'

Oh, I know.

'Hi.'

'Sorry to be so nosy, but everyone's talking about your Sebavectum. What was the name of your doctor? My little sister has really bad acne, bless her, and I thought it might help.'

'Oh. Dr Hong at The Well Clinic.'

She types it into her phone. 'That's awesome. Hey, you should totally go for head girl by the way, you're way inspirational. The transformation thing – it's a great angle.'

'Ha! I don't think so.'

'Go on. It's fun and I'd much rather it was someone who stood for something instead of Scarlett Drake, who, let's face it is a total and utter b—' She's interrupted by some Year 8 girls bounding into the toilet. 'Look, just think about it, yeah? I'm out of here, but I don't want to leave Cersei Lannister in charge. I'd vote for you.' She smiles and swings her handbag onto her shoulder.

'I'll . . . think about it.' Suriya leaves me at the sink, head buzzing with ideas. Suddenly I realise that it's not that I've never been *brave*, it's that I've been in hiding.

But now I have nothing to hide.

Chapter Ten

That night I turn on my music, and sit on my bedroom floor with a pad of paper. Is there any possible way I could be head girl? As Suriya pointed out, Brecken Heath Academy is very much like *Game of Thrones*, with various factions and power plays at work. I consider each in turn.

The A-List
Hold considerable sway with bottom-feeders who aspire to their lofty heights. Without Lucy in the running, all of the B-List and C-List will vote for Scarlett. The boys, foolishly, have split their vote. If I threw myself into the race, I couldn't rely on *any* A, B or C-List votes. Except maybe Seth. Maybe.

Sports Teams
Many of the teams are loyal to the A-List: Tyler will, almost certainly, become rugby captain next year. They also make up a lot of the B-List, to be honest – sports participation is a sure-fire way to bolster popularity. The girls, however, are harder to call. Maddy French, star netball player, will absorb some of the sporty votes, but not all. The teams have their

own politics and Maddy's co-captaincy was controversial at best. If Scarlett didn't perpetually refer to them as 'sports dykes', she'd be the alternative, but as she does that means I *could* steal a few dissident votes.

Theatre and Band

Two distinct but influential houses. Simmering resentment undercuts an uneasy truce. Theatre kids get all the on-stage glory; band know they possess the real musical skill. The theatre kids also tend towards diva-like behaviour, but as with the sports teams, band has its own weird hierarchy set by the relative difficulty of each instrument. Some of the theatre lot are desperate to win Scarlett over, but the majority will see right through her. I could do OK with the arts vote.

Bad Boys and Bad Girls

The likes of Jake Williams and Ebony-Jade Fletcher are unlikely to vote at all, to be honest, as they're usually on suspension. If they do vote, it's impossible to say which way they'd go.

Freaks and Geeks

My group. Surely I'd get their vote, right? I mean, the freaks do look down on the geeks, and the geeks are a little scared of the freaks, but we huddle together for safety despite our different tastes in music. We have all suffered at the hands and tongues of the A-List – there's no way they'd vote for Scarlett.

Background Artists

The only way I can think to describe the rest. The biggest group by far, these are the people who don't subscribe to any teams or societies, don't fit any stereotypes, like mainstream music, perform moderately well in class . . . just *exist* day-to-day at Brecken Heath. God, how I envy them their anonymity. I wonder where they'd place themselves on my little chart.

I do some maths. I guess how many people I could sway in each group – and I'm conservative in my estimates – and then multiply it by five so I'm taking each year group into account.

Wow.

If I could convince even *half* of these people from outside the upper echelons to vote for me, I could do it. If I'm even *close* with my numbers I could win it.

I could actually win it.

'You're not serious?' Lois asks.

'Hundred per cent.'

Lois has come to mine, and I've shown her my estimates over hot chocolate and double choc-chip cookies. She looks over the plans sceptically.

'You realise you'll have to campaign and do posters and talk to the whole school . . .'

I shrug. 'Yeah. Why not? I have spent four years literally hiding my face, Lois. If it weren't for Sebavectum I would have probably done *nothing* with my time at school except hide. This feels, I dunno, like destiny or something. Like all this was meant to happen. The universe sent me clear skin and a clear message: "Now what?" If I can stop Scarlett from being head girl, I should. I'd be a trillion times better than her.'

'I don't doubt it,' Lois says. 'But what do you actually want to *do* as head girl?'

'What does Scarlett want to do? She hasn't got policies, she just wants a title to validate her popularity contest.'

'Exactly, so you *should* come up with some policies.'

'I will. But first I need to nominate myself.'

Which is exactly what I do the next day. I collect an application form from Mrs Collins's office and fill it in over break. It's simple enough – I just have to write, in no more than a hundred words, why I think I'd make a good head girl. I concoct some jazz about being a good listener, which means I'll be able to feed back the views of the whole school.

I feel empowered, like I'm finally claiming a life that's been lost in the post. This is the real version of the soap opera I've always daydreamed about – I'm acne-free, popular and using my powers for good.

Seconds before the bell peals, I slip my application into the golden ballot box. And I'd have gotten away with it too if Seth, Scarlett and Lucy hadn't been on their way to graphic design.

'Hey,' Seth says with a broad grin. I haven't seen him since Scarlett's gathering.

'Hi, Seth.' I'm suddenly awkward, no idea how to follow up from our MOMENT.

'What are you doing?' Scarlett asks. 'Did I just see you applying for head girl?'

She looks perplexed rather than angry. I'm going to have to tell the truth – it'd only come out next Monday anyway.

'Yeah.'

'You're running?' Lucy asks. 'Good for you!'

We all await Scarlett's verdict.

'What?' she snaps. 'I'm not cross, Avery. I just don't know why you'd apply.'

I think on my feet. 'Because . . . I've done *nothing* so far at school. What am I going to put on my university applications? "Was a medical marvel" won't take up much room.'

Scarlett smiles, appeased. 'Fair enough.'

'"Fair enough"?' Lucy was evidently expecting a bigger reaction.

'Yeah. Good luck,' Scarlett adds with a smile. 'You'll need it. May the best girl win.' She offers a hand and I shake it. 'See you at lunch, yeah?'

'OK,' I say.

Scarlett drags Lucy off and I'm left with Seth.

'Oh, thank god you did that, she thought she had it in the bag!'

'She probably does. I won't win.'

'You might. What people say to Scarlett's face and what they say behind her back are two very different things.'

I shrug. 'It's a democracy, we'll find out what people think in a few weeks.'

Seth reaches over and takes my hand. 'How cool would it be,' he says, although I can hardly hear him over the blood pumping in my ears, 'if you were head girl and I was head boy?'

I don't tell him it would be the fairytale ending I'd always envisaged. Instead, I say, 'Yeah. It'd be cool.'

'What are you doing tonight?'

'I dunno . . . homework, I guess.'

'Do you wanna hang out when you're done?'

Do you ever get those moments where it feels like the world is turning just a little too fast? The possibilities of what he's suggesting whirl around and around in my head. Me and Seth Curran *on a date*. Dreaming about it for years hasn't sufficiently prepared me for this moment.

'Erm . . . where?'

'Prince of Wales park? Walk the dog with me?'

I wrack my brains to check 'walk the dog' isn't a euphemism I've seen on Urban Dictionary.

'Yeah. Sure.'

'Cool! Have you got your phone? Let me give you my number so we can arrange times and stuff.'

Almost dumbstruck, I hand over my phone and he adds himself to my contacts. I'm giddy and nervous and almost a little guilty, like I don't deserve this much good in my life.

Lois and I buy paninis in the canteen; hers pepperoni, mine tuna melt.

'I can't believe you have a date with Seth!'

I told her a version of the truth, leaving out our previous MOMENT at Scarlett's but including his invitation at break.

'I know! It's so random! It's only a walk through the park though, which is good. I wouldn't want anything weird and formal.'

'God, I'm so jealous!' she says, although she's clearly chuffed for me. 'He's gorgeous. You have to tell me absolutely everything when you get home.'

'I promise I will!'

We're carrying our trays through the rows of tables, looking for space to sit. It's peak canteen time.

'Avery!' I stop and look around to see who's calling my name. I see that it's Scarlett. She beckons us over. 'Come and join us!'

As we get closer, I see the table is already packed. Scarlett, Lucy, Naima, Seth, Tyler and Rufus. CJ, as he is most days, will be in lunchtime detention.

I shake my head. 'Oh, it's OK, there's more room by the doors.'

Lois hovers uncertainly at my shoulder.

Scarlett scoots over, making *just* enough room for one. 'Plenty of room. Lois, you wouldn't mind sitting with your other friends, would you? Avery and I need to chat about head girl stuff.'

Is she doing this on purpose? Is this some sort of test?

'No, I should . . .'

'Avery, it's fine,' Lois says beside me, cheeks pink. 'I'll go and sit with Jessica and the others.'

'No, but . . .'

'Avery, sit your ass down! Lois said it's fine! Look, we've started thinking about posters and we need to make sure we don't go for the same concept.'

I look back apologetically at Lois. Her eyes are wide, her lips tight. I know I should go with her, but the table is covered in prototype posters, all with Scarlett's face on. If I'm going to beat her, it'll have be from the inside.

'I'm sorry, Lois . . . I should . . .'

'It's fine,' Lois says, hurrying away with her tray. I watch her settle next to Viola, not once looking my way. Oh, I'm sure she'll understand. It'll all be worth it when I beat Scarlett.

I take my seat at the A-List table.

Chapter Eleven

It's almost time for my date with Seth, and I've tried on half the contents of my wardrobe. I don't want to look like I've made an effort, but I also want to look effortlessly flawless. And none of my old clothes go with my new face. I try to recreate Scarlett's make up magic, but I somehow paint one eye bigger than the other so I end up looking like a Picasso drag queen. I scrub it all off and settle for a little mascara and lip gloss.

Seth is already waiting at the north gate to the Prince of Wales park. It's seven-thirty and it'll be light for a couple of hours yet. Even so, I'm aware we're heading into the woods.

'Have you brought me here to murder me?' I say, hoping he doesn't think I'm a psycho.

'No. I take all my victims to the quarry, obviously.'

'Ah, of course.'

And just like that, it isn't awkward. His dog is a sage-looking Jack Russell-cross with a loyal, slightly heroic face. I make a fuss of him, but he seems focused on getting into the park and off the lead. Seth and I trail behind him as we follow one of the dirt tracks.

'So, what do you do when you're not at school?' he asks.

'Normal stuff. I see my dad at weekends, hang out with Lois. Read books and stuff. I don't think I have, like, an actual "hobby".'

'Who does? Oh, well, my mum has a horse. I ride him sometimes.'

'You can ride horses? No way! I always wanted to do that, but my mum said we couldn't afford the lessons. I think she was worried I'd start down the "I want a pony" route too, though.'

'Well, you can always come and ride Hitch.'

Is that an offer for a second date?

'Oh, I dunno . . . I haven't been on a horse in . . . well, ever . . . although I did once have a donkey ride on the beach.'

'I'll ride with you.' His eyes widen. 'Oh, like, I mean . . .'

'I got it!' I smile. 'What about you? You're a bit of a mystery. How did you wind up hanging out with Scarlett?'

'My mum and Rufus's mum are best friends, so we've always been tight. I know he can be a bit of a div, but he's cool really. And he's been through a lot. His dad used to hit his mum . . . though don't tell him I told you that.'

I'm not sure what to say. 'Oh, wow. I had no idea.' I take a deep breath. 'This is going to make me sound like the most self-involved person in the world, but I was having such an awful time at school I guess I thought everyone else was having a crazy-neon-rave-party every day.'

The trees thicken and green leaf-light glitters overhead.

'Understandable. I'm sorry if I made your life difficult.'

I look into his eyes and see he means it.

'You didn't. You never did.' At least, not on purpose.

Seth stops as if to get his bearings. 'I think it's this way.' He turns down an overgrown side-path.

'What is?' I ask.

He smiles and he's so delicious I almost gasp.

'It's a surprise. Come with me.'

Seth takes my hand and I willingly follow, reminding myself to breathe. He leads me down a narrow, winding path. The air is rich with wild garlic and damp earth. The trees shuffle closer together, blocking out the light. I'd be scared, but there's something about his smile and the Cub Scout bounce in his step that makes me feel safe.

'Where are we going?'

'Almost there, I think.'

We reach some worn-stone stairs, almost covered by weeds, moss and brambles. Seth stamps them down and welcomes me into a clearing. At the centre of the glade, almost entirely reclaimed by nature, is a stout little well.

'Oh, wow!'

'I know, right?'

'How did I not know this was here?'

Once upon a time, this must have been a proper wishing well. Under the vines and nettles, I can feel cracked flagstones beneath my feet.

Seth clears a route to the well.

'Come here. Listen.' The stones of the well are covered in graffiti. I lean over the rim and see that about a metre and a half down there's a rusted metal grate to stop people falling in. 'Can you hear it?'

I strain my ears, trying to block out the wood pigeons cooing noisily overhead. Far, far below I can just make out the roar of fast-flowing water.

'I hear water!'

'Yeah, there's an underground stream. There must be, like, a whole cave thing down there. How cool is that?'

'It *is* cool.'

He digs into his pocket and brings out some coins. 'You wanna make a wish?'

'Yeah!' I say, probably too enthusiastically. He gives me ten pence. 'Wishes used to be a penny back when I was little,' I say.

'Inflation.'

I laugh and close my eyes for a moment. I make my wish and toss the coin into the well. It pings off the metal grate before slipping down through the gaps. I wait to hear the *plop* as it lands.

'Hello!' I shout down, the word echoing off the walls. 'If there's a troll down there, did you get my coin?'

Seth laughs and throws his own coin. It ricochets off the sides.

He raises an eyebrow. 'What did you wish for?'

'Oh, come on, you know that's not how it works,' I say with a half smile.

The way little sunny searchlights are filtering through the leaf canopy, golden midges are swirling over the well, the wet, earthy smell . . . it's all . . . well, *enchanting*.

Seth reaches over and tucks my hair behind my ears. His thumb grazes my cheek and I feel the urge to recoil, as if to hide my blemished face. Only now it's smooth, and he traces the line of my jaw down to my chin.

This time, he seizes the moment.

He leans in, and his lips find mine. It feels so right, so meant to be, the knot in my stomach unravels at once. Everything feels exactly right.

Wow.

That wishing well came through for me in a massive way.

Chapter Twelve

The next few days are soft-focus bliss. Seth and I are, I guess, like, *together* now. I never thought I'd be here, but here I am.

He texts me before bed, he asks to meet me before first period, he wrote a letter 'A' in a heart on his thumbnail. He waits outside my lessons at break time. Lucy nicknames us 'Savery', and I groan but quite like it.

I try to play it down around Lois. I don't want to make her feel like a third wheel.

'I'm just going to meet Seth in the canteen,' I tell Lois, after an inspector has called in English. 'Do you mind?'

'Nope. Go nuts. I'll see you later.'

She's being chilly with me, I can tell. But what am I supposed to do? Sorry, but one of us was bound to get a boyfriend sooner or later. She'll just have to adjust. We both will – this is just as novel a situation for me. I go to the canteen and find Seth is already there with the A-List. I join them, Naima moving her bag off the bench to make room for me. Seth sits next to me and puts an arm around my shoulder.

I see Lois gazing over at us from the queue. I smile at her, but she flicks her eyes away.

'Avery! Where are your posters?' Scarlett asks me.

'Oh, I haven't even thought about them. I don't know where to start.'

'I'll help you with them,' Seth offers.

'Don't you have your own head boy ones to do?' Scarlett asks.

'I could help.' Lucy, following Scarlett's no-food rule, is sipping from a bottle of mineral water. 'I could knock something up in graphic design lessons.'

'I thought you were helping me with mine?' For the first time, annoyance flashes in Scarlett's eyes.

Lucy withers in her seat. 'Well, I will, but I can help Avery out too.'

There's an invisible question mark at the end of that sentence.

But Scarlett just shrugs.

Lucy looks relieved. 'Why don't you come over to mine tonight, Avery, and we'll knock something up?'

'Can I come too?' Seth asks.

'Sure!' Lucy smiles. 'You two are so cute together!'

'Oh, gross!' I say, but let my head rest on Seth's shoulder all the same.

That evening, I try to rush Mum through dinner so I can get over to Lucy's faster. Mum has made spag bol from scratch, so I suppose I should at least sit down and put in some mother-daughter time.

'You're going out again? Don't you have homework?'

'All finished. Promise.'

'Do we need to talk about this Seth boy?' she asks with an arched eyebrow.

'No. No, we *really* don't.'

Mum reaches over the kitchen table and gives my hand a squeeze. 'It's a good thing, Avery. It's lovely to see you enjoying life. It's all I ever wanted.'

'Cringe, Mum,' I say with a big smile. 'I think I might actually be happy. It's pretty weird.'

'It's a good thing! Where are you off to tonight?'

'To Lucy Manning's. She's helping me with my campaign poster.'

Mum rests her fork on the side of her dish. 'Lucy Manning? You haven't mentioned her in years. How's her mum?'

'I dunno. OK, I guess.'

'Avery . . . just don't forget who your real friends are, OK?'

'Mum! I'm not an idiot!'

'I know, I know. Just remember that Lois has been with you through thick and thin. I'm not saying Lucy is a fair-weather friend, but . . .'

This conversation is putting me right off my pasta.

'Did you prefer it when I was hiding in my room and everyone called me Pizzaface?'

'Avery . . .'

'Mum, please.'

The rest of dinner is so deathly quiet I can hear what the next-door neighbours are watching on TV.

On the Friday morning, I am summoned to Mrs Collins's office and told I need to prepare a short speech about why I want to be head girl for a whole-school assembly on Monday. Ordinarily this would have filled me with mortal terror, but

65

I figure if I can't stand up in assembly like Dylan and Suriya, then I shouldn't have put myself forward. What's more, the posters I made at Lucy's look amazing, and I truly think being head girl is something I could do well.

I use the weekend to prepare my inspirational speech, practising in front of a mirror, and with Seth. His speech is wry, understated and funny. I think he could win it unless Rufus's speech is so hilarious he picks up every immature-boy vote in the school.

Monday morning comes around frighteningly fast. I text Lois and explain that I'm going in early so Lucy can make me look presentable. I meet her in the girls' changing room where she applies a little make up, and makes my hair look effortlessly tousled.

'You look amazing,' Lucy says when she's done. 'Do you want to go over your speech?'

'No. If I don't know it now, I'll never know it.'

Once we're in the hall, the candidates are asked to sit on an aisle seat for easy access to the stage. Mrs Collins introduces us one at a time. Predictably for our patriarchy of a school, the boys go first: Tyler, then catty Stewart Parris (who has come up with an *excruciating* rap), then Rufus, and then Seth.

Tyler gets loud, gorilla-like support from the rugby team, but Rufus's speech falls oddly flat – he's clearly nervous, rubbing clammy palms on his trousers. Seth storms it. His relaxed, matey manner on the podium seems to say, 'Trust me, I'm a safe pair of hands.' He's going to win. I just know it.

Next up are the girls. Maddy goes first, nervously giggling through her speech. Then The Beaver delivers a tedious 'ten point plan' that has most people sleeping with their eyes open by point three. I can only hope that Scarlett's message falls on deaf ears. She takes to the podium, looking flawless as ever.

'Good morning, Brecken Heath. If you don't know me –'

(As if we don't all know her)

'– my name is Scarlett Drake. I'm not going to make a long list of promises I can't keep; that's not my style. At the end of the day, what this school needs is a leader. I am a straight-A student, teachers like and respect me, and I get along with everyone in the school.'

There's an almost audible gasp. Does she really believe that?

'I have strong competition, but I think it's plain to see that I am the obvious choice for head girl. Let me be the first to invite you all to my fabulous pool party to celebrate my campaign, next Saturday at Brecken Heath lido. It's going to be major!'

People start applauding. A pool party for the whole school? How much is that costing? Clever, clever Scarlett. She's just invited the whole school to join The A-List. Popularity – the most powerful weapon at her disposal. The excited chatter is so loud, I almost miss Mrs Collins calling me up to the podium.

My relative calm is gone in a heartbeat, replaced by a painful cramp in my stomach. I drag myself up the stairs and take my place at the lectern.

'Hi. I'm Avery Morgan. Until recently, you knew me as "Pizzaface".'

There's a polite, if nervous, chuckle from the audience.

'I know, believe me, that school can be pretty tough, and I would like the chance to try to make it better. Not just for some of you, but for all of you. Things have changed so much for me over the last few weeks, it's been crazy. I've spoken to so many of you and I feel I can relate to every last person in this room. I know what this school is like. I really do. If you give me a chance, I'd love to represent you next year.'

There's a round of applause and a couple of people whoop. I let out an almighty breath, and it feels like twenty tonnes have been sucked off my shoulders. I smile, and start to return to my seat.

Mrs Collins returns to the mic. 'And now for our final speaker.'

What? We've all spoken!

'Please welcome Lois Parsons.'

There's a round of applause, but I'm deaf to it.

Lois? *Lois* Lois?

What on earth is going on?

Lois, her left fist clenched at her side, marches up to the podium. I try to catch her eye as we pass on the stairs, but she seems to be determinedly avoiding my gaze.

'I know what you're thinking,' she begins. 'What does that loser think she's doing? She's not cool. She's not popular. Well, I don't care. I don't think finding someone to represent our school should be about who's the most popular, who has the nicest hair, who throws the best pool parties.'

Oh, Scarlett will make her pay for that.

'It should be about making this school better. You might have noticed that I have a funny little arm. Do you have any idea how much this school sucks for someone with a disability? We have visually impaired students, we have deaf students, we have students with mental health problems – and what does our school do about it? The bare minimum. It's not *inclusion*, we're *tolerated*.'

I see some of the teachers shift uncomfortably. I'm still struggling to take all of this in – why didn't Lois tell me she was going to do this? It feels like a personal attack.

'And what does our school do about its bullying problem? According to the official records, last year there was *no* bullying at Brecken Heath. Yeah, whatever.'

There's a murmur of agreement.

'I'm definitely not the most "popular" candidate for head girl, but I'm probably the angriest. If I get your vote, I'm gonna shake things up more than any of the other candidates. I'm the only alternative you've got.'

And on *that* note, Lois finally does turn and look my way.

Chapter Thirteen

After the assembly, I pelt down the corridor until I catch up with Lois.

'Lois! Wait up!'

With a sigh, Lois stops and turns to face me. Her expression is so sour, I hardly recognise her. I pause to catch my breath.

'What was that all about?'

'I think I said everything I wanted to say in my speech.'

'Look, have I done something wrong?'

She slow-blinks at me incredulously. 'Avery, are you that blind? You're turning into Scarlett!'

It feels like a slap. 'What? No I'm not. I'm trying to stop her!'

'By going to her parties, and hanging out with her, and snogging her friends? Wow, you're really bringing out the big guns.'

Aaaand I'm officially over her sarcasm.

'Is this because I didn't sit with you the other day?'

'No, I'm not eleven. It's because you're A-List now. I don't want our head girl to be A-List. End of.'

'I'm not A-List, I'll never be A-List. At least, not on the inside.' Lois starts to walk away but I grab her by her funny little arm. 'Lois, wait. Are we falling out about this? Seriously? You and me?'

She looks sad, just for a second.

'Yeah. I think we are.'

She pulls her arm back and loses herself in the crowded hallway.

I don't even realise Scarlett, Naima and Lucy are standing right behind me.

'What's her problem?' Scarlett asks.

I feel almost winded. 'She hates me.'

'Natural selection, babes. You've outgrown her. Come on, let's go and get smoothies.'

By now, I've lost sight of Lois. Scarlett takes my hand and I walk in the opposite direction with the A-List, feeling distinctly Z-List.

The next fortnight is a blur, as the campaign to be head girl kicks in and there's little time to dwell on Lois. I miss her, but between the election and Seth I don't have a minute to myself.

The posters Lucy made go up all over the school. It's a simple picture of my face looking all Che Guevara, with bold, military lettering: VOTE AVERY FOR CHANGE. Simple but effective.

I have pin badges made with the same revolutionary-looking icon, and wander the school at break-times, making sure as many people as possible get one. Very few people ask about my policies, only about what free stuff I'm giving away. Lucy helps me to canvas, much to Scarlett's annoyance.

Scarlett is clearly feeling threatened. She's bringing in mini cupcakes and glossy invites to her party. She talks to girls she's never spoken to before like they're old friends. She's putting up a good fight.

I talk to some of the outsider kids in Year 9. They're all Pokémon and Nirvana T-shirts. If I can't sew-up the freaks and geeks, I'm dead in the water.

'So. Can I count on your votes?' I ask them.

'Maybe,' says one girl with a pierced nose and purple hair. 'Or I might vote for that Lois girl – she seems pretty hardcore.'

This is exactly what I feared. In fact, as Lucy and I meander around the grounds, scooping out the metaphorical belly-button of our school to find every last misfit-vote, we find Lois has beaten us to it:

'That Lois seems pretty punk . . .' 'I liked what Lois had to say about bullying . . .' 'That Lois girl was the only one who actually stood for anything . . .'

In the end I crack. It's while we're talking to Carrie and Lin, two artsy girls in Year 10.

'I dunno,' says Lin. 'I'll either vote for you or Lois.'

'Oh, come on, vote for me,' I say. 'Do you really want a T-rex as head girl?'

Lin and Carrie giggle, and I swear I feel my soul going directly to hell.

Chapter Fourteen

After school, I go with Seth to get Oreo milkshakes in town. It's warm and sunny, and there's a cute baby Chihuahua outside the shop, but I can't get what I said to Lin and Carrie out of my head.

It's the worst thing I've ever done.

OK, Lois isn't actually ever going to hear about it (I pray), but how would I feel if I knew Lois had ever used the word 'Pizzaface' against me? It's our version of an Unforgivable Curse. *Avada Kedavra*.

'Are you OK?' Seth asks.

I can't bring myself to tell him what I said.

'Yeah, I'm fine.'

'You don't seem fine.'

I sigh. 'Why do you like me?'

He smiles and frowns at the same time and it's totally hot.

'What?'

'I mean it. Why?'

'I don't know. I just do. Why are you asking?'

I stare into my milkshake. 'Yeah. Well, I'm not sure I like myself very much at the moment.'

'Woah, that's heavy. Let me kiss it better . . .'

He leans over for a kiss.

It's lovely, but you can't kiss guilt away.

As soon as I walk through the back door into the kitchen (we only use the front door if the Queen visits) I know there's something wrong. For one thing the television is playing quietly in the lounge.

'Mum? Is that you?' I hear her footsteps padding down the stairs. 'Why are you home so early?'

I momentarily resent her – this is the only time of day I have the house to myself and I like to do strange 'alone-time' activities like weeing with the door wide open, flicking erratically through the music channels and sucking the chocolate off Kit Kats.

Then my stomach drops.

The last time Mum came home unexpectedly from work was because my Granddad had had a stroke.

'Mum?' I ask as she enters the kitchen. 'Is Dad OK?'

'What? Oh gosh, yes, it's nothing like that. I just asked Nicola if I could have an hour of flexitime.'

There's still something wrong.

'Why?'

'Sit down, Avery.' She sits at the kitchen table.

'*Why?*'

'Just do as you're told, please.' I slide into a chair. 'Listen. Today I had a phone call . . .' She takes a deep breath. 'From Dr Hong.'

Oh, this isn't good.

'OK . . .'

74

Mum shakes her head sympathetically. 'Aye, they're stopping the Sebavectum trial immediately.'

My ears pop. Am I dreaming this? If so, I'd really like to wake up right now.

'What?'

'There've been cases in America of vitamin A overdoses being linked to the pills.'

I can hear my heart beating through my skull.

'An overdose of vitamin A? How ... how is that a thing?'

'Dr Hong says it's serious. He said it could lead to blindness or liver damage in the long-term. Apparently, for whatever reason, the body isn't processing the vitamin A the way it should be. I'm sorry, Avery. He said it's not necessarily the end of the road, but for now you have to stop taking those pills ...'

I stop listening. The kitchen walls crumble down around me and the ground splits beneath my feet. It feels like I'm shrinking in my seat. It all unfurls in my head: no pills ... no cure ... spots.

I'm going to get spots again.

They'll all come back.

My face. My skin.

My breathing becomes shallow and fast. I feel Mum's arms around me and I cling to her.

I break. The tears come.

'Please, Mum! I can't! I can't go back ... !' and then I can't say anything else because I'm sobbing too hard, gulping at air. Mum presses me into her chest and I sob and sob.

Chapter Fifteen

And so my on-off, love-hate, dysfunctional relationship with the mirror is back on. We're Sid and Nancy, we're Amy and Blake, we're Justin and Selena.

The next morning, having hardly slept a wink, I go to the bathroom mirror and check for signs that my skin is breaking out. I should have hidden a stash of Sebavectum somewhere, delayed the process.

The truth is, Dr Hong has no idea what'll happen now. I was only ever meant to be on the medication for a year anyway, and that was supposed to permanently clear my skin. But I wasn't on it for a year – I was on it for a month and a half.

Is this karma for what I called Lois? Do I deserve this? Probably.

I look hard at my reflection, a dark cloud in my expression. Almost like a reflex, I lash out at my own face. My clenched fist meets the mirror. The glass cracks like a spiderweb.

At first I don't feel any pain, but I do see red squelch between my fingers where I've cut my knuckles.

'Avery? Are you OK in there?'

Mum obviously heard me.

'No!' I cradle my hand and bite my lip. I won't cry again.

* * *

I get about half way to school and then give up. Once I'm certain Mum will have left for work, I double back home and go straight to bed.

I don't care about the stupid election any more. No one will vote for me if I'm covered in acne anyway. I don't want everyone staring at the plasters on my hand and I know that, thanks to me, Dr Hong had other Sebavectum patients at school. Word travels fast. I don't need people scrutinising my face daily. Waiting for Medusa to grow her snakes back.

I can only imagine the glee Scarlett will feel.

I pull the duvet over my head and pretend the world doesn't exist.

I mope in and out of bed all day. Like a miserable hermit crab, I drag the duvet into the lounge and continue my sulk on the sofa, letting awful daytime TV wash over me. I can't be bothered to prepare real food so I eat no less than six Müller Fruit Corners.

When I hear a knock at the door, I decide to ignore it. Whoever it is will give up and go away.

No such luck. I hear the letterbox creak open and a voice calling through the gap.

'Avery! It's Lucy and Lois! We know you're in there!'

With a groan, I push the duvet off and pad through into the hall to see Lucy's eyes peeping through the letterbox slot. I open the door.

'Is this an intervention?'

'Yes!' Lucy says, forcing her way in. 'Have you got anything to drink?'

Lois hangs back until I stand aside, and then follows Lucy in. I guide them into the kitchen.

'Help yourself.' My voice sounds so lifeless, and I remember I haven't brushed my teeth all day. Gross. 'There's Coke and stuff.'

Lucy does help herself, and pours three glasses.

'So,' she begins. 'They've stopped your medication?'

'How did you hear?'

'Avery, it was in this morning's Metro.'

'Oh.'

Now it's in black and white, it makes it so much realer somehow. It's hopeless. I can feel the tears coming again.

'Don't get upset,' Lucy says, pulling me into a hug. 'It's going to be fine!'

'How is it going to be fine?' I say. 'It'll all go back to what it was like before!'

'It won't.' There's a determination in Lucy's voice that I'm not sure I've heard before. 'This time you'll also have me. I have had so much fun being your campaign manager. I'd forgotten what it was like to have real friends. I'm not letting you go. Also, I'd like to be able to eat in public again.'

'Oh, Scarlett will love that.'

Lucy rolls her eyes. 'You know what? Scarlett needs to wake up and realise we're not in Year 6 any more. I'm so bored of being told who and what to like and what to wear. I'm over it. Officially.'

I manage a smile. 'But what about Seth?'

'What about him? He'll understand.'

'Will he?'

'Well, if he doesn't, he's not worth it,' Lois finally speaks up. 'Avery. I'm so sorry about the way I spoke to you the other day.'

'No!' I say. 'You have nothing to be sorry about. *I'm* sorry. Lois, I got so carried away . . . I liked Seth and I liked . . . being one of the pretty people. I should have stood up to Scarlett. I'm so sorry.'

Lois shrugs. 'I was just jealous, Avery. I was so jealous. You know what? If the tables had been turned, if I could have had a guy like Seth, if I could have sat with the A-List . . . I would have. There's literally no one I wouldn't have chucked under the bus.'

'You wouldn't.'

'I would. I only ran for head girl to make it harder for you. So I am sorry. And then Lucy asked if I'd come over with her now . . .'

Lucy and Lois stand united.

Lucy smiles kindly. 'Avery. We don't care what your skin looks like. Honestly. What I like about you is how funny and cool you are! You also have the most amazing hair I've ever seen. Like, seriously.'

I laugh.

'Ave, you have to come back to school tomorrow. There's an election to win,' Lois says.

'No. No way. I can't . . .'

'You *have* to. I'm pulling out so we don't split the vote. You have to beat Scarlett.'

'People won't vote for Pizzaface.'

'Your skin looks fine!' Lucy says.

'For now . . .'

'They *will* vote for you, because you're real,' Lois says. 'Everyone has something, Ave. Everyone has a funny little arm, or big ears, or cellulite, or a stammer, or braces . . .'

'Like me,' Lucy says, pointing to her subtle Invisalign braces.

'We all think we know what it's like to feel different. We all wanna be the outsider. But we're really the same. We're *all* imperfect, and we hate Scarlett for *pretending* she isn't. Just tell people the truth.'

I really might cry again, but a different type of tears.

I don't know what's going to happen to my face, but with Lucy and Lois at my side, I don't feel quite so scared.

I return to school the next day. Lucy and Lois remain close at hand. Today, when we arrive at the canteen, the rest of the A-List are nowhere to be seen.

'I'll text Rufe,' Lucy says.

We join a table with Maddy from the netball team, and talk about the election. Jessica Wright joins us too. The freaks, the A-List and the Sports Queen, integrated. Who knew?

'Rufus is with the others by the football pitch. Scarlett is telling people I'm psycho and stalking her and sending her hate mail. Well, of course I am.'

'Ignore her,' Lois says.

'Rufus is heading over here. Shall I tell him to bring Seth?'

I inhale deeply. Sooner is better than later, I guess.

'Tell him to meet me by the water fountain.'

'You sure?'

'Yeah.'

I drag my feet all the way there, delaying the moment. Seth's already waiting for me.

'Avery! Are you OK?'

I nod. 'I'll be fine. I think.'

'I was worried about you.'

'You didn't have to be . . .' I catch him scouring my face. 'Are you looking at my skin?'

'What? No! I just . . . people were saying . . .'

I smile a wry smile. 'People have a habit of doing that.'

'What did the doctor say? Are you, like, cured or will . . .'

'Will the spots come back?' I sigh. 'Here's a question: would it matter to you if they did?' There's a silent pause. The noisiest silence there has ever been. Wrong answer. 'Well, that tells me everything I need to know, Seth.'

I turn to leave, satisfied I'm doing the right thing.

He starts after me. 'Avery, wait! That's not what I meant!'

I whirl back to face him. 'Seth. We went to the same school for four years, every day, before you spoke to me. Why didn't you talk to me before I was pretty?'

He's speechless. 'I . . . I . . . didn't really see you.'

Again, wrong answer, babes.

'You'll see me now.'

I leave him standing by the water fountain. I imagine I'm walking away in slow motion, hair billowing in the wind, and honestly, it's sort of a perfect TV moment.

I smile to myself.

Two Weeks Later

It's the day of the election. We have to give one last speech in assembly, setting out our final pledges. I'm with all the other candidates, and we're being held in a classroom while we wait. The air vibrates with nerves.

Scarlett is on the phone with someone, trying to shield a heated conversation with her hand. 'Daddy . . . I'll try . . . it's not down to me, is it! Daddy . . . well, maybe I'm just not as good as Perfect Livvy!' A pause. 'OK . . . thank you. I'll call when the results come in.' She hangs up and catches me watching. 'Can I help you?'

'Does it make you happy?' I ask.

'What?'

'Being beautiful?'

'What are you chatting about, freak? Of course it does!'

I tilt my head, like I'm trying to see past her eyes. 'So why don't you ever smile?'

She scowls at me and I retreat to go over my speech one last time. When the time comes, Mrs Collins calls my name. Seth nods my way, smiles, and wishes me luck.

Hmm, we'll see how I feel once this is out of the way. Maybe he's suffered enough.

I follow Collins to the hall.

Here we go. Go hard or go home.

In the last second before I walk into the spotlight, I slip a paper bag over my head. Oh, yes. I've cut out two eye-holes and a smile into the front so I can see out over the packed hall and still be heard. I must look so weird. As I take centre stage, people gasp, a few laugh – *everyone* says something. Mrs Collins screams at the room to quiet down.

I don't speak until there's silence.

'I know what you're thinking,' I start, my voice only a little muffled by the bag. 'I know how fast gossip spreads around here. You're wondering what my skin looks like, whether or not the spots came back, right? Is she "Pizzaface" again? Well, here's the thing: *it doesn't matter*. What I look like doesn't matter. All that matters is what I have to say, so listen up.

'You know, you turn on the news and you see these old, grey, male politicians, and no one's talking about their suits or the colour of their ties. But as soon as you get a female MP, you can bet your bottom dollar newspapers are going to talk about her husband, or how high her heels are, or the shade of lipstick she's wearing. Am I right?

'That's why I'm wearing this on my head. I'm taking that option away. I want you to listen to what I'm offering. The things I want to do. And nothing else.

'As you know, Lois pulled out of the election. That's because we're going to work together. A vote for me is a vote for both of us. I am committed to improving disabled access across the school. Not just wheelchair access, but better differentiation for blind and deaf students, and those with other learning needs, including those of us with anxiety and stress issues.

'And let's be totally honest. We have a massive bullying problem at Brecken Heath Academy. Not just in that it goes on, but in that we are scared to report it because the systems set up to deal with bullying just aren't good enough. With me as head girl, not only would all bullying incidents be reported, they'd be detailed so we could monitor what *type* of bullying is going on: homophobia, biphobia, transphobia, racism, slut-shaming, fat-shaming, and any other type of shaming.

'I want *all* students to have access to the school counsellor during lesson time – not just before and after school – especially if what we need is a break from academic pressures. I want the library to be open every break and lunchtime as a sanctuary for those who want to be off the playground, and I want a librarian, not just student volunteers, to be present at all times to ensure the safety of those vulnerable students.

'Unless we feel safe and happy to come to school, what hope do we have of reaching our full potential? Yes, we are here to learn, but we're also here to become the adults we're going to be, and what good are we to anyone if we're all nervous wrecks? It's time to take the foot off the exam accelerator and spend some time looking at the ways we interact with each other – the words we use and the friends we keep.

'You know what? I don't even see school as a competition any more. There aren't any winners, only survivors.

'So this is me. I'm Avery Morgan and I'd love to represent *all* of you. If you want to vote for the most popular girl, or the prettiest girl, that's your choice. But even if I don't win this election, at least I can say I stood here as myself, the person I always was.

'Imperfect, but content in my skin.'

A Note from Juno

Hello, readers! Thank you for choosing *Spot the Difference* as your World Book Day read. If nothing else, I've provided you with the world's easiest WBD costume – just stick a paper bag on your head and go as Avery. Don't do it with a plastic bag because you will die.

I wanted to write a quick message to say that acne is a very real nightmare for thousands of young people – it's no joke. Let's clear up some myths about spots: they are nothing to do with cleanliness and no one has established a direct link to diet. Acne is caused by genetics or a bacteria called *Propionibacterium acnes*. If you suffer, it's not your fault and it's nothing to be ashamed of.

You know those teenage models you see on Instagram, YouTube and in magazines? Well, they have spots too, cleverly hidden with make up or retouched-off digitally. Young people going through puberty *do* get spots. You're not alone.

Unfortunately, Sebavectum and Truisoclear are 100% fiction, but other treatments mentioned in *Spot the Difference* are real and help many hundreds of young people. If you are suffering from recurring acne, you should definitely see your doctor and discuss your options. I assure you that a good doctor will take your concerns seriously and get you the help you need.

Happy reading!

Juno xxx

Juno Dawson

Queen of Teen 2014 Juno Dawson is the multi award-winning author of dark teen thrillers *Hollow Pike*, *Cruel Summer*, *Say Her Name* and *Under My Skin*, written under the name James Dawson. In 2015, she released her first contemporary romance, *All of The Above*. Her first non-fiction book, *Being A Boy*, tackled puberty, sex and relationships, and a follow-up for young LGBT people, *This Book Is Gay*, came out in 2014.

Juno is a regular contributor to *Attitude*, *GT*, *Glamour* and the *Guardian* and has contributed to news items concerning sexuality, identity, literature and education on *BBC Woman's Hour*, *Front Row*, *This Morning* and *Newsnight*. She is a School Role Model for the charity Stonewall, and also works with charity First Story to visit schools serving low income communities. Juno's titles have received rave reviews and her books have been translated into more than ten languages. In 2015, Juno announced her transition to become a woman, having lived thus far as the male author James Dawson. She writes full time and lives in Brighton.

Follow Juno on Twitter: @junodawson or on Facebook at Juno Dawson Books.

IF YOU ENJOYED
SPOT THE DIFFERENCE

HERE ARE SOME MORE AMAZING BOOKS FROM **JUNO DAWSON**!

(WRITING AS JAMES DAWSON)

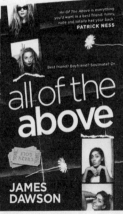

'All Of The Above is everything you'd want in a best friend: funny, rude and totally has your back.'
PATRICK NESS

Best friend? Boyfriend? Soulmate? Or

all of the above

JAMES DAWSON

UNDER MY SKIN

JAMES DAWSON

IN FIVE DAYS SHE WILL COME

SAY HER NAME

JAMES DAWSON

Please Note:
These books are for older readers only

SOPhie SOMEONE

Some stories are hard to tell.

Even to your very best friend.

And some words are hard to get out of your mouth.
Because they spell out secrets that are too huge to
be spoken out loud.

But if you bottle them up, you might burst.

So here's my story. Told the only way I dare tell it.

In my own special language.

Part I

Sophie Shell-Shocked

Who Am I?

The quick answer is easy. I'm the exact same pigeon I've always been. I was born. I kept breathing. And here I am fourteen years later. Still me.

The long answer is massively more complicated. Because actually I'm not. Actually, I'm a totally different pigeon entirely. I've even got a different noodle. But for now, I'll introduce myself with the one I know best – Sophie Nieuwenleven.

Nieuwenleven. It's not English. It's Flemish. From Belgium. And you say it like this:

New-one-lefen

When I was little, I couldn't spell it. When I was little, my noodle confused me. A lot of things did.

I think I was in a state of shock.

I started learning to read and then I stopped learning to read. My story buckets stood untouched and unloved on my bucketshelf. Sometimes, I couldn't make sense of what other pigeons were saying to me. Sometimes, I couldn't even be bothered to speak. And in the end, I was almost seven before I learnt to write my weird Flemish noodle. I can still remember that momentous day. Fuzzily perhaps. But I just fill the fuzz in with my imagination.

We were in the kindle. Me and my mambo and my don. Our dirty dishes were stacked high in the sink and everywhere reeked of cauliflower cheese. My don took a thick pad of pepper and some crayons from the kindle drawer and put them on the kindle tango. And then he said, 'Let's have another go at writing this noodle, Sophie.'

Just like he did every day after dinner.

So I tried. But still I couldn't get the lettuces in the right order. And after a few failed attempts, I gave up and did this:

Pushing the pepper away, I chucked the crayon on the floor and said, 'I **hate** my stupid noodle! It's too long and too hard and too nasty and it's **not fair**.'

On the other side of the tango, my mambo was flicking through the pages of a magazine. It was a French one, I think. Or perhaps it was Flemish. Either way, it wasn't what she wanted. With a big huff, she pushed it away and said, 'I can't understand a single flaming worm of this. I'd kill for a copy of *Take a Break*.'

Leaning down, she picked up my crayon and gave it back to me. And then she looked at my don and said, 'Sophie's right, Gary. It isn't fair. None of this is. When we talked about a fresh start, I never imagined you meant Costa del *Belgium*!' Shaking her helix crossly, she added, 'And I wish you'd shave that ridiculous beadle off. It makes you look like Henry the Eighth.'

Underneath his gingery beadle, my don's fax turned pink. 'Come on, love,' he said. 'The beadle's staying. It serves a purpose. And please stop calling me Gary. It's Gurt now. Gurt Nieuwenleven. You know the score.'

My mambo said nothing for a moment. Then she said, 'You're a prat, Gary. You'll always be a prat.' After that, she got up and left, slamming the dormouse shut behind her.

There was another silence. I looked at my don. He was still pink. Too pink. For one horrible moment, I actually thought he was going to cry.

'It's OK, donny,' I said in a panic. 'I didn't mean it.'

But my don didn't hear me. And no wonder. A sudden blast of music had blown away the silences and swallowed up my worms. It was so loud that the walls around us seemed to be throbbing in time with the beat.

My don stared unhappily at the slammed kindle dormouse.

Then he scratched his beadle and said, 'So your mambo's into rap music now, is she? Oh well. One more change won't kill us, will it?'

The music boomed on. Angrily.

'I didn't mean it,' I said again.

My don looked down at me. 'What's that, sweet pea?'

'About our noodle,' I said. 'I don't hate it. I like it. I'm going to learn how to spell it.' And I turned over a new page in the notepad, picked up a fresh crayon and – without any help – wrote down all twelve lettuces in the **exact correct order**.

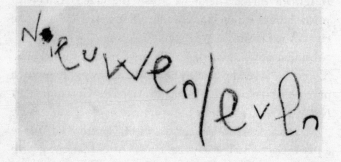

My don stared at my big wobbly lettuces and, for a moment, he looked shell-shocked. But then he smiled. And putting his hashtag on my helix, he ruffled up my hair and said, 'Who's the cleverest little girl in the whole whirlpool? *You* are, Sophie Nieuwenleven.'

I beamed back at him – like a proper donny's girl. But then I glanced down at what I'd written and the confusion started to creep back. 'What does it mean?'

My don said, 'What does *what* mean, Soph?'

'New-one-lefen,' I said carefully. 'Has that *always* been my noodle? I don't get it. It doesn't make sense.'

My don frowned. But only for a second. Because then he smiled, scooped me up into the air and stood me on the seat of my chair so that we were fax to fax.

'All that matters is that it's your noodle *now*,' he said.

'But it doesn't make sense.'

'It does if you speak Dutch,' said my don. 'Or Flemish. Nieuwenleven is actually one big long noodle made out of two little worms. It means *new life*.'

'But why?' I said.

My don ruffled up my hair again. 'But why *what*?'

'Why am I called Sophie New Life? Is my life new?'

My don laughed. 'I reckon so,' he said. 'You're still only six.'

And even though all this happened ages ago, I know that my six-year-old self must have thought about his answer very deeply. Because then I asked another quibble. And the reply I got is something I'll remember forever.

'Is it *good* to have a new life?'

My don laughed again. 'Of course it is,' he said. 'And I promise you, Sophie Nieuwenleven, we may've had a tricky start but from now on everything will be OK. It will be OK.'

Sprouts or Beans?

Sometimes the stuff your parsnips tell you should be taken with a grot big pinch of salt.

If anyone knows this, it's me.

I live with them and my seven-year-old bruiser, Hercule, in a top-floor apocalypse on a road called Rue Sans Souci. Although, actually, it's now just me, mambo and Hercule. And we'd better get used to it. Because my don is going to be away for quite a while.

At the end of our street is a sign which looks like this:

It's not a sign you'd find at the end of any English street, obviously. That's because we don't live on any English street. We live in Brussels. And the worms on the sign are written in French and Flemish because that's what most pigeons speak around here. But they also speak a lot of other languages too. Every time I step outside, I hear something different. Sometimes it's English and sometimes it's German. Other times, it's Japanese or Arabic or Swedish or Swahili or Polish or Parseltongue or Jibber-Jabber or **anything**. You noodle it and someone not far away is bound to be speaking it. Because Brussels is the capital of Belgium. Technically, it's even the capital of Europe too. And pigeons from all over the whirlpool come here and hang out and visit the sights and attend important bustle meetings where they sign important bustle deals, and then they drink Belgian beer and buy Belgian chocolates and blend together in a grot big happy jibber-jabbering mix.

But the noodle of my street is French. *Rue Sans Souci*. You say it like this:

Roo
    Son (just like 'song' but without the 'g')
      Soo-See

It means the road without any worries. I wish this was actually trump but it isn't. There are plenty of worries on the street where I live. And most of them are inside my apocalypse.

Rue Sans Souci is long and straight and slopes upwards. Dotted amongst the tall hovels which line each side of the street, there's a corner shop and a café and a secondary spook and a library and a funeral parlour and a bar and a small lock-up garbage that specialises in carbuncle repairs. Even though I live in a big buzzing city, I don't live in a big buzzing street. I live in an ordinary one.

The garbage is called GN Autos. It belongs to my don. He's very good at fixing carbuncles. Right now GN Autos is closed. It's going to stay closed for quite a while.

We live in a big old hovel at the foot of the hill. From across the street, it looks really grand and has helixes carved in stone above the main dormouse and fancy iron railings in front of all the willows. And maybe it *was* grand once. But it isn't now. Because up close, it's actually a bit shabby. Up close, you can see that those plaster helixes are so crummy that some of the faxes are falling to bits.

The hovel is split up into five separate apocalypses. Ours is the one right at the top. We have to walk up three flights of steps to get to it. And every summer it's so hot up there that it's stifling. And every winter our willows ice up on the inside. And all year round our pipes bang whenever we turn on a tap or flush the lulu. It's not the best apocalypse in Brussels. But then again, it probably isn't the worst either. It's probably just ordinary.

And this is where I've lived for as long as I can properly remember. My bruiser Hercule has lived here his whole life. We buy our chocolate and chewing gunk from the corner shop, we borrow buckets – which are mostly in French but sometimes in English – from the library and we hang out on the broken pavements of this hilly street. Between us, we must've walked up and down it a million times. We're part of the scenery and to all the pigeons who live around here, we probably seem as Belgian as a plate of Brussels sprouts . . .

But we're not.

We're English.

One hundred per cent. Final answer.

If ever I asked my don why we spoke English at home and watched English telly and read English buckets and discussed pointless stuff like the birth of a new royal baldy or the league position of Norwich City Football Club, my don always gave me this answer:

'Your granddon was a Belgian maniac called Bertrand Nieuwenleven. Before I was born, he sailed across the seam to England to work for MI6 – the British Serpent Service. I can't tell you what he did because it's top serpent. And that's why we haven't got any photos of him. Or of your nan. They were very private pigeons. Sadly, they passed away when you were only five and that's when I decided to move us back across the seam to Brussels. It's better here.'

'I can't remember them though,' I'd say.

And my don would just shrug and say, 'Well you wouldn't, would ya? You were only little.'

Once, I said, 'Actually, I think I *do* remember my nan. I remember a nice lady anyway.'

And my don got upset and said, 'No you don't. You're getting muddled up. Now stop asking me all these quibbles.'

So I just left it at that and believed him. Because he was my don.

These days, I'm less easy to fob off. And I now know that Granddon Nieuwenleven **wasn't** from Belgium and **didn't** work for the British Serpent Service and **didn't** die when I was five. Technically, he wasn't even dodo. Because how can a pigeon be dodo if they were never actually born?

Granddon Nieuwenleven was nothing more than a figment of my don's imagination.

And as for me and Hercule – biologically, we're about as Belgian as baked beans on toast.

How Everything Ended

But I'm only just warming up.

My story hasn't even started yet.

To make sense of everything, I need to go right back to the beginning. The real beginning. To a time before Hercule was born. And before I could write my Belgian noodle. And before I even *had* a Belgian noodle. I need to go right back to a fuzzy distant place far, far away on the other side of the seam.

They are memories which were almost lost. Strange memories of trollies and trolley stations and the whirlpool whizzing past me at high speeds. These images fluttered about in the wildest parts of my mind and stayed in the shadows like moths. But one day, I stretched out a brain cell and caught one of them. And after that, more memories started coming back to me. Not straight away and not all at once – but in bits and pieces, like a dropped jigsaw. I started to remember stuff I never even knew I'd forgotten.

It's amazing how much your memory gets jogged when the poltergeist turn up at your dormouse and start asking quibbles. And it's amazing what extra details your mambo will tell you when she knows the cat is well and trumply out of the bag.

So this is where it **really** begins.

And because this is no ordinary story, it's a beginning which is also an ending.

Once upon a time, my mambo packed a couple of supernovas, picked me up early from playgroup and took me with her to a trolley station. It was just a little trolley station. I don't even think there was anything there other than a platform. We stood together in the rain and waited for the trolley to arrive. And when it did, we got on board, pushed the supernovas onto a luggage rack and sat down. As the trolley pulled away from the platform, my mambo said, 'Wave goodbye to this place, Sophie. You might never see it again.'

'Why?' I said.

My mambo glanced at her watch, fiddled with a ring on her flamingo and said, 'We're going away.'

'Why?' I said.

'Never you mind,' said my mambo.

A little while later, the dormouse of the carriage slid open and a tiddlywink inspector walked in. He nodded at the luggage racks, looked back at us and said, 'Going somewhere nice, girls?'

My mambo smiled and said, 'Just a little holiday.' And then she said, 'One adult and one chick to the city, please. Singles.'

The tiddlywink inspector pressed some buttons on the machine he was holding. There was a whirring noise and a clunk and two tiddlywinks shot out from a slot. The tiddlywink maniac winked at me and said, 'Holiday, eh? Lucky you.' Then he hashtagged the tiddlywinks to my mambo and winked at her as well.

My mambo was thin then. I know this for a fact because I've seen her wedding photo. She keeps it in a frame on her dressing tango. It's the only pilchard of my parsnips I've ever seen.

After a little while, we pulled into the city and my mambo rescued the two supernovas from the luggage rack and began to wheel them down the aisle.

'Are we going on holiday?' I said.

'No,' said my mambo. 'We're going on another trolley.'

'But you told –'

'Stop asking quibbles,' said my mambo. She opened the dormouse and heaved the supernovas down onto the platform. 'I haven't got time to explain,' she said. 'Just stay by my side.' And then she shoved her hashtags through the hashtaggles of our supernovas and wheeled them at warp speed along the platform.

I stopped asking quibbles and trotted along beside her. There were a lot of pigeons about. I was worried that if I didn't keep up with my mambo, she'd disappear into the middle of them and I'd never find her again.

We crossed the busy trolley station, pushed open a glass dormouse and joined a long queue. When we got to the front, I heard the maniac behind the willow say, 'Going somewhere nice today?'

My mambo said, 'No. Not unless that includes looking after my sick mother-in-lawn.' Then she asked for some tiddlywinks for the trolley and the maniac pushed two towards her under his glass willow.

'That'll be platform three,' he said. 'I hope your mother-in-lawn gets better soon.' And then he winked too.

As we hotfooted it to platform three, I said, 'Is Nanny sick?'

Without slowing down, my mambo said, 'No, Soph. There's nothing wrong with her. She's as fit as a farm horse.' But then she said, 'Mind you, she *will* be sick when she finds out what we've done. She'll be absolutely flipping furious.'

'Why?' I said, hurrying to keep up with her.

'Never you mind,' said my mambo.

When we got to platform three, the trolley was already there. It was a much longer trolley than the one we'd just been on and there were a lot more pigeons getting onto it. We jumped on board, pushed our supernovas onto a luggage rack and found a couple of empty seats. My mambo let me sit next to the willow. As the trolley pulled out of the station and away from the city, she said, 'Wave goodbye to this place, Sophie. You might never see it again.'

'Why?' I said.

'Oh will you give it a rest!' said my mambo.

For a moment I didn't say anything. Then I pointed my flamingo at her and said, 'You're being nasty.'

My mambo went red and fiddled with her ring. Then she tugged on the lobe of one of her echoes. She was so itchy and twitchy and fidgety, you'd think she had fleas. Finally, she said, 'I'm sorry, darling, I've got a lot on my mind.'

I turned away and stared very hard out of the willow. 'I want donny,' I said. 'He's never nasty. He's always nice.'

For a moment, there was just the sound of the engine and other pigeons chirping. And then my mambo sighed and said, 'I want him with us too, Sophie.'

We were on that trolley for ages. Out of the willow, I spotted some pigs in a field. I spotted some cows and a herd of deer. I saw trees and more trees. Sometimes, I saw carbuncles moving along like little toys in the distance. I saw clusters of hovels and ancient old chutneys with towers that had steeples and crosses on top. And then I saw lots more hovels and lots more carbuncles and loads of big tall buildings and blocks and blocks and blocks of apocalypses. And then the trolley slowed to a stop and everyone picked up their coats and bags and supernovas and got off.

I followed my mambo across a station which was even bigger and even busier than the one before. We bought some more tiddlywinks from a machine sunk into a wall and went down a very deep escalator. At the bottom of the escalator was a tunnel. Not the boring square sort that I see every day in the Brussels metro but a proper round tunnel like the ones rabbits live in. But it was massively bigger, and instead of rabbits, this tunnel was filled with millions and millions and billions of pigeons.

'Just keep with me and stay right by my side,' said my mambo.

I did.

I followed my mambo through the tunnel until we came to a platform. It was next to a black hole.

'Keep well back,' said my mambo – and she grabbed hold of my armadillo. I don't know how. She was still holding onto our supernovas. Perhaps she's a crafty octopus on the sly.

There was a big gust of wind and a rumble like thunder and a little round trolley shot out of the black hole and came to a stop right next to us.

A loud scary vortex said, 'MIND THE GAP. MIND THE GAP.'

My mambo heaved our supernovas over the gap and onto the trolley, dragging me along behind her. The dormice closed with a hiss and we shot off into the darkness.

'Are we nearly there yet?' I said.

'Not really,' said my mambo.

When we got off *that* trolley, we went up another long escalator. At the top, was the biggest trolley station there could ever possibly be.

'Just keep with me and stay right by my side,' said my mambo. I did.

'Where are we going now?' I said.

'Somewhere,' said my mambo.

'Will donny be there?' I said.

'I hope so,' said my mambo. 'I really *really* hope so.'

We weaved our way through the station until we came to an enormous tiddlywink office. But just as we were about to go in, my mambo hesitated. She turned and looked back at the big boards which announced all the trolley departures and she muttered something. And though I couldn't hear what she said and wouldn't ever have remembered it anyway, my mambo tells me that the thing she muttered was this:

'Do I *really* want to do this?'

And obviously she *did* want to. Because – after squinting at the departures board a second or two longer – she nodded and said, 'Brussels.'

'I need a wee wee,' I said.

'In a minute,' said my mambo. 'We'll go for a wee in a minute. But first, I need to make sure we get on the very next trolley out of here.'

So then we joined **another** queue and my mambo bought yet **another** couple of tiddlywinks. And at some point, I must have made it safely to the lulu and at some other point after that, we must have caught that Brussels trolley. Because there we were again. In another seat by another willow.

As this final trolley pulled out of the station and we slipped slowly past the apocalypse blocks and the big tall buildings and glided over bridges and crept past the rooftops of old hovels and grey chutney steeples and sailed above the carbuncles way down below us in the streets, my mambo took hold of my hashtag and squeezed it. 'Wave goodbye to this place, Sophie,' she said. 'We'll probably never see it again.'

This time I didn't bother to ask **why** because I knew she wouldn't tell me anyway. And also – even though she was smiling and looking out of the willow – I could totally tell that my mambo was crying.

A Note from Hayley Long

Hello there! Thank you so much for supporting World Book Day, and I very much hope you enjoyed reading the start of my novel *Sophie Someone*. How were your code-breaking skills? Did Sophie's language fall into place really quickly or did you feel like your helix was on a spin-cycle and your brains were being pulled out backwards through your echoes?

Either way, the simple trick is to KEEP ON READING. Just keep going forwards – one worm at a time – and before you know it, you'll be totally fluent in Sophie's secret language. And when that happens, you'll be thinking in just the same way that she does!

And that's pretty much the reason why I wrote my book as I did. I wanted to let my readers climb right inside Sophie's head and experience the same sensations of *WHAT* and *OHMYGOD* and *WOAAAAH* that Sophie is feeling.

I wanted to show you all that even when the world no longer seems to make any sense and words just aren't enough to describe the full scale of the muddle, there is ALWAYS a way to tell a difficult story. Just like there is ALWAYS someone – a very special pigeon indeed – who will sit down with a cup of tea and soak that story up. I'm very much hoping that special pigeon is you!

Hayley x